CW01566963

You Are The Friction

Published by Sing Statistics

Printed by Oddi, Iceland

Cover by Ray Fenwick

ISBN: 978-0-9569295-1-8

10 9 8 7 6 5 4 3 2 1

YOU ARE THE FRICTION

Contents

Illustrations → Stories

Stories → Illustrations

Foreword

Just to be clear: Yes, I've read this book. I read the whole thing. I read it twice. You could say I luxuriated in it. I relished it. If this book is a banquet, I feasted on it. If it's a bath, I bathed. If you are figuratively hungry, figuratively dirty—I advise you to read this thing! Read it right now! Read it like you'd read a sky full of fireworks.

Of course I received this book as a PDF, because the book doesn't exist yet. It is strange to read a book like *You Are The Friction* on a computer. It is so booky a book: perfect typeset pages, handwritten titles, twinned images and text. Not some digital flimflam, thin as liquid crystal—this is wood-pulp, glue, ink. This is a beautiful thing that people have slaved over, and made, and now that it is in the world it can be lost, found, discarded, treasured, kept in safes and thrown in graves and inscribed, with a pen, to lovers.

This is how *You Are The Friction* works: Jez Burrows and Lizzy Stewart, who sing statistics, asked twelve different writers to write stories. Then a different artist 'illustrated' each one of these stories—a picture for each tale. Meanwhile, each of the twelve artists also drew a separate picture, imagined out of thin air. The writers received these pictures and then 'illustrated' them, with stories. So: twelve pictures inspired by twelve stories, and twelve stories inspired by twelve pictures.

These stories and pictures are connected by method, not by theme. They are all very different. The throughlines are accidental, coincidence. Why do several stories feature beards, baths, or epic-length book series? I do not know. Why are there multiple references to lawn chairs, stray eyelashes and sex with flatmates? Don't ask me. Nobody colluded. We must all look inward, to our collective unconscious.

Perhaps you wish to know which are the best stories? I can't tell you that, I really can't, but I can say that Craig Taylor's "The Person Who Came Before" is gorgeous and astral, the best kind of ghost story; Toby Litt's "The Writer" is like JD Salinger snorting milk through his nose; Evie Wyld's "Why Are You Awake?" is an insomniac familiar; Tess Lynch's "Matryoshka" is bruised and cold, and like an empty wardrobe, and is a portrait of newlyweds; Kevin Fanning's "Cell Phone Heart" is so fragile, so fragile, a parent's story sent from the near-future; and Ronnie Scott's "Sex Map" is roughly human, comic, clear as glass.

As for the pictures, I could say some things but it is probably easier for you to just flip through these pages. (e.g., look at the careful wonder of Hannah Waldron's drawing on pg. 52.) Sometimes the images and the stories are parts of the same universe. Sometimes they are two sides of the same coin, or two conversations happening in the same room. Sometimes the images reveal and other times they conceal and sometimes they make you laugh because the faces are silly. Or they seem like reflections of each other.

But an illustration is never really a reflection. The pictures of stories, the stories of pictures: these are interpretations, tellings, magic tricks. An illustration is necessarily a lie: it is never the thing itself. Twelve of these stories are lies about pictures and twelve of these pictures are lies about stories. Twenty-four truths, twenty-four fictions.

There is an abundant intimacy to illustration. I learned this when I wrote a story for Sing Statistics' second collection, *We Are The Friction*. Lizzy's drawing made me feel as if she had opened my story up, like a wardrobe; like she had undone the clasps and pulled open the doors, and looked at its dark interior. When it was my turn to illustrate—when she gave me a picture and I had to write its story—I stared so hard at that image. I turned my ear to the page and listened. I wanted to work out what the drawing dreamed.

Partnerships are fragile. They last as long as they last. In amassing these pages, artists and writers traded something. They traded and made, wrote and drew, and when they were finished they sent files across the ether, JPG or DOC or PDF, and they were collected into a book. These aren't just little trifles, confections of character and image and Jennifer Love Hewitt references: they are the remains of partnerships, proofs of puddings, what's left after the intimacy has passed, and you look up from your desk, and the light's not quite as you remembered it.

I hope you enjoy every dot and line.

Sean Michaels
Montreal, October 2012

Illustrations → Stories

Illustrated by Scott Campbell

Written by Joshua Allen

Cordwood Ollie lights his pipe and notices his hands are trembling, which is serious business for lumberjacks. It means one of two things:

1. He is too far from the trees, and forgetting himself, or
2. His time amongst the trees is coming to an end.

He shakes the match out and, before realizing what he's doing, tosses it to the floor. It smokes there inside a coil of heavy cable. Ollie looks away, ashamed. Never would've done that in the woods. Seen too many black, dead pines thanks to some yokel throwing a ladies' cigarette into dry needles.

The producer slaps a friendly hand on Ollie's shoulder and he barely feels it. Absolutely no strength in it at all. The producer says: "Big scene today."

Ollie nods, trying to disappear into his thick black beard.

"Gonna be super," the producer says. "They nailed it in rehearsal."

Ollie says: "Everyone's doin' a real nice job. But."

The producer leans in close. "When they're showing the Best Picture nominees," he whispers, "*this* will be the clip. *This* will be the moment."

Ollie looks out onto the set, bustling with lumberjacks and trees and woodland creatures. Every last one of them brought in from the forest that runs along Fort Hook's eastern border. He knows every face, every growth ring, every whisker, but the looks in their eyes terrify him. Their happiness, their enthusiasm at being involved in *the pictures* feels to Ollie like a ridiculous lie that everyone's agreed to believe. I mean look over there at Three Finger Dan, holding the boom mic as best he can, laughing that laugh. His gimpy little hands are trembling, I bet. Sure, he's yukking it up now, telling jokes, winking at the actresses, eating donuts from craft services, but tomorrow he'll wake up in a dark motel, here in a city—a *desert* city, of all things—and he'll realize he's no longer a man. No longer a citizen of the timberland.

He definitely won't be no lumberjack. Him or me neither. Orders are barked through mechanical horns and Ollie winces. The crew quiets down, people get settled. The director has a hushed conversation with the actors. Lights are adjusted. Three Finger Dan hoists the boom on his broad, meaty shoulders. Somebody says *OK people*.

And the scene begins, and the log hands the pink animal a bouquet of flowers, and she has tears in her eyes, and it's just how Ollie saw it, the moment that told him there was something even more vast than those woods, something that the world needed to hear about, something he wrote down that night in his childish, untrembling hand.

Somebody says *OK good enough* and the crew bursts into life again. The set smells of coffee and flannel. Three Finger Dan comes over and claps Ollie on the shoulder and it hurts like it should.

"First eighteen beers are on me," Dan says.

"Beer here tastes like breast implants," Ollie says.

"And how!" Dan says.

Ollie heads for the exit, relighting his pipe. He doesn't shake out the match before dropping it to the floor.

Illustrated by Oliver Jeffers

SIGHTSEERS

Written by Joe Meno

Made in BELFAST →

And then a funny thing happened: both of Vida's legs were terribly, terribly broken. It was just outside the airport at Stansted. The gigantic backpack was throwing her off balance and she was not paying attention because she was talking to Adam, asking: are you okay? Do you still feel airsick? And so she had not noticed that the black cab which she was now walking in front of was also moving as well. She had been so excited by the drama of the trip that all physical motion and positive feeling seemed indistinguishable; though in the exact moment of the accident, she did happen to take notice of the rigid, open-mouthed expression of horror on Adam's bearded, wide face. The rubberized, front passenger tyre rolled over both of her legs, breaking the fibula of her left, and the tibia of her right, before stopping with a squeal of its brakes, and everything after that was to be conjecture in conflicting insurance reports. Decently, Adam held her hand until the ambulance arrived, mumbling words of encouragement; but it was hard to take him seriously, even with the look of genuine concern plastered upon his face. It was because Adam was always *so Adam*, a bit dorky, with that dumb brown beard and unibrow, always mentioning things he remembered from Hebrew school, or whistling songs from some out-of-date musical nobody had ever heard of, but he was nice, and a real friend, which was the reason, even after two years of knowing each other and working at the same non-profit radio station, nothing was ever going to happen. Also, he was a Jew and not the least bit embarrassed about it and Vida had some pretty weird ideas about the inner workings of the world of Jewish men: were they all circumcised or was it just some of them? How could you tell who was and who wasn't? It was hard not to think of Adam's

penis as also having that same greasy brown beard and somehow wearing a very small yarmulke. But maybe that was just
her imagination getting carried away again.

Later, she was in a hospital in London, in a sea-blue backless
gown, her legs imprisoned above her in plaster casts, staring
up at the ceiling at a pair of cracks that looked a little like
George Washington crossing the Potomac. The backpacking
trip—five countries in four weeks—was obviously doomed.
So Adam cashed in their *Eurail* passes and managed to get a
refund on part of their airline tickets, and the decision was
made to try and get a flight to Belfast, where they had a
friend, Veronica, who was also an American, and who had
a spare room and a spare bed where Vida could recuperate,
while still enjoying the soft thrills of Europe. Their friend
Veronica had quit her job at the radio station back in Ohio
and had moved to Belfast for a man, but the affair had not
lasted. Still she had landed a job at the public radio station
in Belfast, and they let her do book reviews on the air, which
was more than she had been doing back in the States, so she
had decided to stay on. The plan was then officially changed
and Vida and Adam agreed to spend their remaining time
in Belfast, where Veronica had even gone so far as to borrow
a wheelchair from another girl at work. The wheelchair had
belonged to some girl's mother, who had had Parkinson's
and had passed away the year before; Vida looked forward
to sitting in the chair and putting her hands on the rubbery
wheels, feeling the soft marks made by the hands of someone who had died so recently. This thought was a little childish as were a few others; it was silly to enjoy all this attention
but at least she was aware of how stupid she was being.

The plane landed in Belfast at George Best Airport without incident; exiting the airport terminal this time, Vida made a big show of looking both ways before crossing the pedway to the parking garage where Veronica—who had become more thin and lustrous than anyone remembered—had a rusty-looking station wagon parked. It was only mere minutes however, driving back along the motorway, before Veronica broke down in tears, claiming she had never been more lonely in her life, living in this foreign city, with its history of bloodshed and its charmingly gruff citizens. Vida, who had both her legs extended across the backseat of the station wagon, was happy she did not have to see Veronica's face as she was crying. Before they arrived at her flat, Veronica announced that a friend from hers at the radio station had told her about a rave that night and did they want to go? She hadn't done anything fun in months and was counting on the two of them to try and cheer her up.

"But my legs are broken," Vida said.

"Yes, but we've got the wheelchair," Veronica said, a little too brightly, nodding towards the folded-up device in the rear of the station wagon.

"But do people even have raves anymore?" Vida asked.

"Of course they do. This is Europe. The club scene is still very popular here. Except all the kids smoke plant fertilizer now. Or maybe they eat it. Come to think of it," Veronica said, "I'm not sure exactly."

Vida glanced at Adam and shrugged her shoulders.

"You two can go, if you want," Vida said. "I don't think I'd be much fun."

"Well, I wouldn't think of going without you. Which means you have to come," Veronica said, laughing, and there was something about Belfast, or living in Europe, that had made Veronica much more confident, much more sure of herself, which, considering it now, Vida was not sure she liked. They opened the rear of the station wagon, got the haunted wheelchair out, and positioned Vida in it. She felt like an actress playing a role; people, walking up and down the small stone street, looked at her as they passed, and for the first time in her life, Vida had to acknowledge how attractive being tragic seemed to be.

The rave, or "rave", was held in a loft somewhere, beside somewhere, down the street from somewhere. From the backseat of the station wagon, with the yellow lights of the city drifting by, it was hard for Vida to tell she was even in Europe. The loft was a longish space with a number of otherworldly-sized speakers placed at odd intervals throughout, and, for some reason, there were a number of stripped mattresses left lying around as well. Maybe it used to be a mattress store, and then thinking it, she realized it had been. The mattresses now seemed to be condominiums for a variety of insects and rodents, and wheeling past a stack of them, it was hard not to consider the more lurid aspects of the evening; with the techno music leaping from speaker to speaker, the torn, chewed-up mattresses, the young people in bright neon eighties gear, who had probably only ever heard about raves before tonight. Everyone was dancing and acting like it was a good time, except for Vida, who, from her chair, began to sulk. Of course, no one at this spazzed-out party, with its repetitive, droning music, under the cloud of a now-active smoke machine, was going to notice how beautifully tragic she looked.

But then someone did. A girl, maybe sixteen or so, wearing a formal plastic frock, teetered over to her, looked down at Vida's broken legs, at the puffy off-white plaster casts, and leaned in close with a voice that sounded like Vida's grandmother's and breath that smelled like peppermint Schnapps: "I just graduated," she said, pointing to the grey plastic gown.

From what? Vida wondered and tried to look away.

"I'd like to sign your cast," the girl said. "How come nobody's signed it yet?"

Vida sighed and it was then that she saw the alarmed expression on the girl's face. Before she could ask, What's wrong? the girl leaned over and vomited a bright green amalgamation of Schnapps, vodka, fast food taco meat, and a substance that may or may not have been horse tranquilizer. This marked the immediate end of the rave for the three American friends.

Back at Veronica's, Vida decided she would not begin speaking again until she had a bath. She got her blue sweat pants down—which were splattered with vomit—and changed into one of Veronica's robes. The problem was she had to wrap the casts in plastic bags and she knew she wasn't going to be able to do that and get into the tub by herself. Veronica had left the apartment to go and get something else for the three of them to drink, but she had been on her mobile phone with her boyfriend before she left, which led Vida to believe their friend was going off to pay her ex a visit first, and so, rolling her eyes as she said it, just so he wouldn't get the wrong idea, she asked Adam to help her get into the tub. He agreed and then wheeled her into the small bathroom, forcing the wheelchair beside the old iron tub with its four claw feet.

"How do you want to do this?" Adam asked awkwardly, eyes fixed on the ceiling.

"You've got to wrap my legs like the doctor said."

"Okay."

And he went about doing that for several minutes.

When he was done, still looking up, he asked, "Now what?" and she sighed, blowing a few rogue strands of blonde hair from the front of her face.

"Now you got to turn on the water and help me in."

"Okay."

He turned both taps on, and let the water warm up, before crawling around behind her, reaching his two hands under her armpits, and lifting. It was rough going, Vida trying to balance, Adam not wanting to grab her too violently, but finally, he got her standing beside the tub.

"Do you want me to take your robe off?" he asked and knew as soon as he said it, she was not even going to dignify the question with an answer. She sighed again and he helped her right leg over, then her left, and she slid down into the tub with a weird, blubbery sound, the robe darkening as it got wet.

"Let me know if you need anything else," Adam said and before he could go, she had to call out for the soap, and he nodded and reached for it by the sink, offering her a small white bar that looked like a piece of ivory. Adam placed the bar of soap in her small wet hand and it was then that he did something neither one of them would have ever expected: he placed his hand between her legs, under the water, just beneath the folds of the now-soaked terrycloth robe. And then, sensing her confusion, and something of her weakness, he tore off his jeans and shirt in a flash—keeping on his white underpants—and then he crawled in on top of her.

If this story is to have an ending, which it should, it will end in one of three ways:

1. Vida and Adam will sleep together—having intercourse —on Veronica's gold and green sofa. In the morning, Veronica will still not have returned, and so they will stare at each other with continued longing, sharing a cup of tea in a cup decorated with the Virgin Mary and a burnt piece of toast.

2. They will have sex in the bathroom and it will be awkward and then try again an hour later on the sofa and it will be pretty terrific but Adam will ruin it by talking, talking, talking endlessly about not being first chair clarinetist in his temple's youth jazz ensemble, at which point, the affair will be definitely, un-regrettably over.

3. The sex will be neither good or bad and will therefore be immediately regarded as a mistake and then a silence, a lull will fall over them for the rest of the trip, until, flying back to the States on the airplane, a rumble of turbulence will force Vida to grab Adam's hand, and remembering the boyish softness of his pink palm, she will, without thinking, place it against the flat part of her chest. Thump-thump. Thump-thump.

Illustrated by Rob Hunter

THE WRITER

Written by Toby Litt

We had his house completely surrounded by then. The guy didn't do shit that we didn't know—and when I say shit I mean shit. One of our grad students was ready every day for his morning's evacuation, which tended to happen between 7.15 and 7.20AM. When he left to attend his mother's funeral the year previous, we lifted the top off of his front lawn—every shaggy blade of grass from edge to edge—without making a single cut in it—and we re-routed the drains out of his residence. Did all this, mind, *at night*, without any of his neighbours waking up and hearing or seeing anything. Not that Donald would ever've spoken to them to be informed of any of this stuff. (I say neighbours, but the closest was a farm three hundred metres away.) When the media called him a recluse, that didn't mean he made an exception and invited the mailman in for cookies at Christmas. His blinds, which had curtains behind them, and duct-taped garbage bags up half the window before them, had not moved once in the six years I was stationed there. And after the Internet brought a new universe of home delivery into existence, Donald had never found it necessary to leave the house. This residence was your standard white wannabe White House, isolated behind trees but surprisingly close to the turnpike, and if you wanted to see what anti-capitalism in action really means you should've taken a look at the peel on that paintwork. The man did not require fresh air to keep him going (something we should, perhaps, bear in mind in our on-going investigations). What he did require, his groceries, have been laboriously itemized, analyzed. Tinned corn made up the basis of his diet, that and burnt toast. The grad student who monitored his bowel movements, via the flush pipe, estimates in his since-published PhD that

ninety eight percent of Donald's excreta contained traces of
carbon and corn. We had become increasingly anxious that
the great man was in his diet missing out on certain crucial
vitamins, minerals and other trace elements. After a conference including all the senior faculty, we decided that some
intervention was necessary. If Donald were to become ill, his
productivity—never less than six hundred words finished a
day—might, at that crucial stage, be undermined. Donald,
you see, was almost into the final chapters of Book Seventeen of the series—the culmination of his entire life's work.
Alarm bells—and I do mean alarm bells—I initiated a panic
button two years ago, after he had his first fall—alarm bells
rang when the grad student found blood in Donald's 7.19AM
stool sample. We immediately sent it for analysis at the University labs; they cleared their schedule to receive it. By evening, we had our answer. Donald was suffering from a condition whose name was so complicated that I have never been
able to remember it, though I can still to this day recite the
first Chapter of Book One without flaw, semi-colons and
all. That morning had been perfectly normal for the master.
At seven, he was drinking black coffee with his burnt toast.
We monitored electricity usage within the house, and each
appliance had a signature of power drainage. Toaster. Kettle. In the final year it had gotten to the point where we
could remotely tell the difference between keystrokes on the
laptop. Tragically, he only ever used this for emails, sticking
to the sainted Underwood for all drafts of the work. I hear
you wondering how we know for sure he achieved six hundred words per day? Well, of course we had the entire house
bugged. Lasers were trained on each window, with four in
total on his study—this was at the rear of the property, high

in a small attic roof with mansard detailing. Four so that we had two primaries, separately analysed, under controlled conditions, in total isolation one from the other, and two back-ups. Donald's typewriter, bless it, gave a ding whenever it reached the end of a line. Counting the number of dings per day was idiotically simple. Any undergrad could have done that. What the cryptography and audio-analysts were able to do, between them, was reconstruct the words Donald had almost certainly written. As he hadn't published in thirty years, we had no way of checking our output against his input. Statistically, in trials on another typewriter back on campus, recorded blind through glass, we achieved ninety-eight percent accuracy. The loud upwards clunk of the carriage told us when he was creating a capital letter. He seemed to relish the skirr of the carriage return level—either to create his usual two-line section break or at the deserved end of yet another page. The transcription mistakes that remain usually occurred when Donald subsequently worked the typewritten draft over in pencil. We knew that he occasionally used a brand-name correction fluid. Our last year's annual faculty get-together coincided fortuitously with a major order by Donald of stationery. Because we'd had a mole working at his supplier since the previous year, we were able to isolate his online request and all be there in the distribution centre to lovingly pack up the reams of 100gsm paper, the typewriter ribbons, the dozen erasers. Those who wanted were able to kiss the points of his yellow pencils—though we drew the line (forgive me) at allowing one grad student to take a pencil off with her to the rest room. I am fairly certain I know what Karen was planning to do. The scent would, quite possibly, have blown the entire operation. (Karen's scent was noticeable.) Everything that was done on that day was entirely respectful of Donald's person and his project. We returned full of elation, worried only that the undergrads who had been deputized to person the monitoring equipment in our absence wouldn't have screwed up. When it became clear that they had done a fine job of *not touching a single damn thing*, we celebrated with champagne. And when the stationery supplies were delivered the following morning, I think I can speak for the entire Humanities Program when I say we'd never felt closer to Donald. But then, in the last six weeks, first with the blood in the stools, and then with the decision to intervene in Donald's diet, a real mood of dread began to overtake the whole Live Author Study Team. I mean, all apart from the work itself, we had a considerable funding investment here. Donald was the jewel in the crown of our department's research portfolio. At yet another interdepartmental meeting, the possibility of introducing supplements into the tinned corn was dismissed as impractical. It would involve taking over the factory, to doctor the corn as it went along the production line. The loaves seemed the obvious place to put vitamins, etc, but some research done by the Chemistry & Biochemistry Department collaborating with the Medical Nutrition College in anticipation of this concluded that one of the reasons Donald so liked burnt toast in the first place was that the carbonization blitzed just about any residual nutritional value out of the foodstuff. Lord, he'd looked whiter than any man I've ever seen the last time he opened the door to retrieve the left-behind-by-arrangement stationery boxes. His stoop had increased—hardly a surprise, given the hours per day he spent bent over his Underwood. With corn and bread ruled out, we tried first of all with a free gift of some carefully selected Vitamin supplements added to his week's groceries. (The grocery boy is ours.) We had never done anything so extreme before, but this was life and death stuff. Donald put the supplements in his trash immediately, and they were retrieved by an M.A. student who had been helping out all that summer. I have the rejected vitamins on my desk now, alas, along with ten empty cans of corn. (Pretty much everyone in the Faculty has a corn can collection somewhere or other.) Donald also drank Coca-Cola, from cans, and ate other things, from cans. Tuna, hot dogs. He was really a slob, if you ask me. His first wife says he used to enjoy good food and fine wine in the 1950s, before he met the woman who became his second wife, and was turned ultra-left-wing-radical by her. Whiskey went in, too. Two bottles a week. Donald was seventy-five, of the age when two bottles per week was pretty solid going. In the end, the free gift ruse having failed, we decided the simplest thing to do—an expedient we'd also always avoided before—was to tamper with the water supply. I realise now that this was ethically suspect. But you have to understand that there were faculty up for tenure, faculty with cute kids I've met at cook-outs, men and women and kids whose lives would entirely have gone splat had Donald ceased meaningfully to produce. We estimated, at around the time that the supplements were first introduced into his mains water supply, that Donald had five or six weeks to go before he completed Book Seventeen. Looking back now, those seven preceding years seem golden times. We would spend our evenings in the hide, reading and rereading the master's day's output. What would happen to Nasrat's trompe l'oeil castle? How long could Adalbert's treachery go unnoticed by Viktor and the Three Burgesses? Where had the second crust been hidden? And then, as I'm sure you're aware by now, the alarm bells rang once more. The typing began, as usual, that morning, September 4th—I'll never forget the date. But as the first rough transcripts began to come through, we realised something was seriously wrong. Instead of continuing the narrative, beginning top left of the page, Donald set out for a letter and wrote, *Dear Whoever-You-Are, I know what you're up to. I've known for some time. I'm not stupid, you know. (Of course you know.) The vitamins were insulting—as if I wouldn't know they were from you! And the lawn operation, you must know, was clumsy in the extreme. But now even a child would know that the water tastes different for a reason. I do know what I'm doing in here. I know exactly. I expect the vitamins were a response to what we both know is the bad sign of blood. And now that you know I know I expect you'd like to know what I'm going to do. Well, I'll let you know. Yours, Donald.* And, after that moment, the subject typed no more that day—which was terribly disconcerting. The clatter, clatter, ping had been the soundtrack to our lives. Looking back through his Internet activity, subsequently, we can see that recent news reports must have made Donald aware of advances in surveillance technology. His typewriter, those final days, was used mainly to send us taunting messages: *I know how the story ends, but you're never going to know* and *It was only knowing that no-one would ever read it that enabled me to write it. If you don't know this, you know nothing* and *there are a number of major things you don't know.* We anticipated, as one distinct possibility, a suicide attempt. What we had no way of predicting was that he would on September 20th open his front door, step through it without even a cloud-wards glance, walk off through the trees without locking up. He was carrying nothing but an axe. The detonation of the house three minutes later came as an even greater shock—causing permanent hearing damage to all four of the study-window listeners, that being where the bomb was planted. As I say, we were completely unaware that Donald had retained any materials from his more militant sixties days, nor that the chemicals were un-degraded to the extent they could be used. We were accused at the latest MLA of failing to pay sufficient attention to Donald's sudden use of an alarm clock. We, as I freely admit, were unprepared for the immense violence of Donald's departure. At the most, an attempt at conflagration had been anticipated. We had plans in place for that. The Fire Department were good to go. Instead, in the confusion that followed the house's de-struction, Donald was—I admit, I admit—able to make his way to the turnpike, flag down a passing vehicle and make what has been called his Great Escape. English Departments across the country have been notified of his disappearance and, I can assure you, that the slightest whiff of burnt toast will bring the full weight of real-time academic scrutiny down upon him once more, whatever backwoods he may be hiding out in. A man like Donald has habits. A man like Donald cannot change.

Illustrated by Maxwell Holyoke-Hirsch

Written by Nicolas Burrows

Pierce sat in the recording booth, smoking a brown cigarillo and holding out the script in front of him as if it were on fire. Ice cubes popped and clinked in a glass of brandy on the small table beside him. This was supposed to be a good career-move for him, his agent had said. Besides, it had worked for Morgan; he had won an Oscar for his voiceover work.

He took a long languorous sip of the brandy and dragged on the cigarillo, the flavours mingling in his throat like honey. He was ready. A whale swam majestically through an expanse of cold dark blue.

"He rises upwards, his hulking body moving like a huge blue muscle towards the surface, where he must go if he wants to breathe; if he wants to survive."

The producer behind the glass partition showed a thumbs-up to signal a good take, but he knew it wasn't one of his better performances. He was out of his depth. This wasn't like playing James in the hugely successful franchise that had secured his fame. And anyway, he fucking hated the sea.

Pierce thought about all the other actors that he had shared the screen—and sometimes a bed—with throughout his long and illustrious career. Pretty and naive girls covered in sand. Young cocky actors with greased heads who would treat him as a mentor on and off set. Friends he'd shared lewd stories with over a brandy, and father figures he had watched and learned from as a fresh-faced and ambitious novice. He looked at the next clip of a fat sea cucumber on the screen. These were his co-stars now; stupid, ugly spineless blobs, wriggling fish and obnoxious sharks. Despite his disgust he managed to read the line with a little more panache.

"A Spanish Dancer, so-called because of its resemblance to a flamenco dancer's billowing skirt"

The producer didn't give a shit about the quality of the narration. Pierce knew he wasn't giving one-hundred percent. And yet it was proof of his mastery of the craft that he could still sound convincing enough for the idiot behind the glass. *And probably for the idiots watching the fucking thing when it got broadcast.* But who would even appreciate the undulating timbre of his carefully rehearsed, disconcerting Anglo-American voiceover? You were never the star of the show with these things. Morgan had said so. You were always playing second fiddle to the million shimmering shapes under the waves.

And Pierce despised them. He was frustrated and he was getting old and he missed the thrill of explosions, of exotic locations and of beautiful women sprawled across linen. He felt the weight of his swelling belly pushing at his belt. His eyes were dark and shrank back behind a hundred tiny folds of skin when he smiled. And every day new valleys appeared on the tundra of his once-taut forehead. He didn't care about the ocean. He didn't care about mantis shrimps or stingrays or those bloody dugongs with their watery eyes, snuffling up the sea floor.

It definitely feels like the end of something, he thought, stubbing out the cigarillo. He reached over and lifted the glass to his lips, but all that passed them was a thin, unsatisfying trickle of brandy-tainted water.

Illustrated *by* William Exley

Written *by* Ronnie Scott

I heard the last two travellers I would need slowing down along the ridge.

I untwisted a fish lined V of corks on my Akubra.

Travellers reliably drove up here on a tour of Australia's Big Things. This was a set of one hundred and fifty objects that were scattered around Australia, which Wikipedia called "loosely related"; the loose relationship, not to wreck it for you, was that they were all sizable objects. Victoria had a lot of them, and New South Wales had forty-three, including the Big Axe, the Big Blue Heeler, the Big Banana, the Big Bunch of Bananas, and even—this constructed in support of the reuse of waste water—a one-by-five metre Big Poo. The numbers were healthy in every state, yet it still was thought of as a "Queensland thing", and people drove up Queensland's rear with especial priority.

Last decade, the government introduced a second design of Queensland number plate, giving residents the option of displaying that they lived in "The Smart State" or "The Sunshine State" (as before). I display "The Smart State" because there are fewer of those, and if I drive south to Brisbane, I often otherwise have trouble locating my nondescript vehicle.

Queensland is home to forty-nine of Australia's Big Things, including three Big Crocodiles and two Big Crabs. One of the crocodiles, at nearly nine metres, is a scale impression of a crocodile named Krys the Savannah King that was shot in 1957.

I am near the Big Golden Gumboot, an eight-metre fibreglass statue that is named for a competition between the towns of Tully, Innisfail, and Babinda to see which is the wettest town. Babinda has recorded more rainfall than Tully in the last forty years, but the Big Thing itself was built by Tully's Rotary and Lions clubs in Tully, in 2003. Its height commemorates the highest rainfall Tully ever got, which was in the clean-break year of 1950.

It probably being cheeky enough to have an unwon statue, the sign at its foot just says, concessionally, "Tully—A Pretty Wet Place".

As the frogs, slick millions, who croak me into sleep will all attest.

Two corks on my hat had wound together, but they unwound easily once I set them into backwards motion. The upside of fishing line is that it's slippy and strong. The downside is that once it knots, it's absolutely knotted. This one hadn't, but.

The girl who came through the door to my cottage was the sort of girl the gang of boys who'd stayed last week would have called "a bit chunk", and she'd responded to her body opposite to how she should have. She'd covered up as much of it as she could possibly have covered; in the heat, this resulted in sweaty rivers down her ribs, and when she decided to get comfortable and took off her black cardie, I saw red scatters on her arms; other people may have mistaken those for arm-pimples, but I knew, living in the north, this was a fungal problem.

Her boyfriend had only rounds of muscle and wore just nothing at all, moving through the world as though he wished he could wear less. They dumped their bags in the guest annex, and I knew they'd be back out. But I'd been running my B&B long enough to just go about my day. I

set up at the pub counter, removed my shoes and read a pro-
file on my laptop of Julian Assange. The pub was really my
kitchen, which I'd done in dark, varnished wood, between
some of whose joins I'd installed a long, low, glass-doored
drinks fridge—in many minds, that was all that made a
kitchen an establishment.

A rarer type of traveller up here had an interest in the badlands. The "horror stretch" of Australia was the Rockhampton Mackay floodplain. A portion of the Bruce Highway
was dotted with these poor and gang-tagged settlements
that'd had the life worn out of them by the dread of drought,
and a spray of murders that led one writer to consider it an
"immense historical crime scene". Since the 1970s, camping
couples had been found sniped in their sleeping bags; other
couples dead and separated, one shot in a car; children had
gone missing, mostly girls, of course; and Aboriginals of all
ages had been used for their black bodies, and then slaugh-
tered because they may have thought to talk. At points along
the horror stretch, enthusiasts were able to locate reddish
smears at the old kill-sites, though many of these would
have been from animals.

My little B&B didn't lie along the horror stretch, really,
but Queensland, which was Smart and Sunny, had never
been the clearest of states. Mackay, for example, at the
stretch's northernmost extent, was usually thought to lie in
north Queensland; it was certainly *like* it qualitatively, with
the skies like microwaves, swaying with convection as high
as the eye could see. Yet it was served governmentally by
both Rockhampton and Townsville, which were central and
northern Queensland, respectively.

The farther north you got from Brisbane, the closer you

always were to some kind of frontier, either a dead one, like the mining towns, or for many travellers, one that felt wholly, paradoxically fresh: here, folks could look at your girlfriend's sweat-slickened thighs like they were figuring out whether it was worth the unaccustomed way they glistened, when they thought about how tough they'd be to grip. It sure felt like the badlands still, to the rareish interested couple, and besides, once you had passed Mackay, Cairns just made it worth continuing.

There were nude beaches in Cairns where travellers just cooked up their bodies.

As a person who grew up here and came back here will attest.

Carson had driven this way to experience the horror stretch, whereas Jessie and her fungi had simply seemed to love the guy, though she'd been frustrated with the time he had spent "fingering peg holes". She said this last thing shortly before stumbling to her room; it had been early evening before they'd come down to the bar, flush-faced with rodgering or showering or both, and she'd made light work of a ham-cheese sanga and quadruple its calorie-count in xxxx beer. After she left, there was a silence while I rinsed the sandwich plate. "She got bit," Carson eventually offered. "By some ants. At the killing site. While I fingered the old tent peg holes. Or I don't know that they were tent peg holes. They were wedged-up maybe, and cakey. But they were definitely ants that bit her. Big black ones."

"Bull ants. They cane."

"They seemed to. She doesn't complain about much," he apologised. I wasn't comfortable with his critique of the girl.

Apart from a few bad comments, she hadn't been aggressive. What she clearly had been was a bit drunk and unhappy; this didn't need apology in my book. He yawned his legs open, like his groin was a slick hinge, and scratched both his balls up the pant-legs. The thing that made it slightly likeable, rather than plain disgusting, was that it was clearly gormless and unintended. Carson asked me about checkout, and I said it was whenever.

"That's kind of you," he said.

I said, "It's bored of me."

"What's good bushwalking around here?" he said. "A place we went to in Victoria had a koala corridor, all above us these koalas."

"I've got a glowworm corridor. All around you, these glow-worms. Take you out there with a light and turn your light out. And you'll see 'em."

"Oh," he said, enchanted. "Jessica would love that."

"Will she get up early, then?"

He looked for his watch, and saw instead his watch-tan.

"Tell you what," I said. "I'll give you a wakeup knock at… five? That way we'll have an hour before the sun really rises, watch the glowworms go out while it does."

"Oh," he said, imagining, "that would be the best."

He told me some things they'd done on their drive around the centre and then into sugar country, up here. He hadn't liked Brisbane, and, as I'd gauged him an exploratory man, I told him of Jurassic Lake, a lake on rarely-patrolled air-port land, which fish had fallen into due to rare king tides at some point, where they'd grown to rare sizes due to agricul-tural waste. You could get to there by canoeing a creek, and then carrying the canoe for a kilometre or two.

People say that there are country houses with no locks on them, but that is bullshit, I have never seen one. I locked the cottage and shut reception down, leaving on a golden light that would help the guests feel more at home here than it's natural, in a guesthouse, to feel. The safety of stewarded space, the dead nature of public space, and the knick-knackedness of a country home, it all resulted in a complexity that only added up correctly if the complexity was entirely unseen. This was my aim here. I propped myself in bed against a hardy stack of pillows and cracked open the most recent of my leather-bound diaries, filling it, as usual, with lies and counterfactuals: that my name was Solomon Samuel, bush ranger, in a future world that had forgotten the bush-truths, and it was my right to restore this via broadsword. It was volume four of an epic that I kept myself amused by. Tonight, when I dreamed, I dreamed about my girlfriend. We were travelling in the tray of a nondescript vehicle. She turned to me and woke me up alarmless with a smile.

A tropical storm had spilled down several hours before I woke them, and Jessica said she felt, at certain times, as we were walking, that we were descending through the half-pipes of God: long, concave, and soil-damp, these natural northern corridors, with moss-pads planted at all possible points. "Hold your flashlight on your feet some," I said, "it's God's game to twist an ankle." She was nice sober, yet I enjoyed the quiet minutes that the glowworms required before their lights hummed on around us all.

We enjoyed the lights for long enough. The best discovery was Carson's: one clump of worms that glowed bravely enough that he could see each glowworm's texture against the others', right there in their thick.

Then the sun was blueing out the glowworms. They saw it. "Where next?" asked Carson.

"I don't know," said Jessica. "I think that was all I had to see."

"What about around here? What's around here?"

"Nothing," I said. "There's nothing around here. Some strawberry farms, another place like mine."

"No Big Things," Jessica said.

The reasons people come here and the reasons people live here do converge at points, there are an awful lot of those; I love, like they love, the golden sun, and I love, like they love, the dawn's wet woods, and it fascinates and interests me to be left here on my own, where there is always time to bake damper and read profiles of Julian Assange and Wiki-How anything.

Illustrated by Jim Tierney

Written by Ned Beauman

The first time I met the Dragon, he was pounding on the drinks machine by the conference room so hard I thought the glass was going to smash. "What the fuck have you done with my fifty pence?" he was shouting. I got his attention and then introduced myself.

"We're going to be working together," I said.

The Dragon gave me an incredulous glare and then followed me into the conference room. He wore a stained wool sweater and his grey beard was strangely uneven, as if it couldn't quite get a footing in the flab of his jaw. We sat down. "You must have been a bit apprehensive about this, I suppose?" he said.

I wasn't sure what he meant. He was rumoured to be impossible to work with, yes, but I couldn't see why he'd bring that up. "Why?" I said.

"Well, you know what they say. Never meet your heroes. Never, ever meet your heroes."

"Oh," I said. "Yes." But the Dragon wasn't one of my heroes. I'd never read a single one of his books. In fact, I'd never read a fantasy novel in my life. Ever since I was a teenager—not 'insufferably precocious', as the phrase goes, just boringly precocious—I'd been reading Beckett and Blanchot, because I wanted to write like Beckett and Blanchot. (Unfortunately, no one wants to read novels any more by people who write like Beckett and Blanchot, which is how I ended up writing scripts for computer games.) But my boss must have told him I was a huge fan. I'd read somewhere once that when American intellectuals visited the Soviet Union in the 1930s, it was always arranged that everyone they met, even the waitresses and the railway station porters, should have read all of their books. They never seemed to see through the ruse, and that, more than anything else, was why they were happy to go home and extol Stalinism to their friends.

"So what exactly are we knocking together here?" said the Dragon. "I've got an idea for something about a mad ice witch who tears men's souls to shreds."

"It has to be about a dragon."

"Why?"

"The game's called *Dragonblade*. In the first seven levels you defeat all seven hierarchs of the Dragon's cult, then in the eighth level you fight the Dragon in his cave."

"No. Tell those morons to get rid of that."

"It was in place when you signed the contract. They've already programmed most of it."

"Well, I'm not having my name on anything so fucking trite. I have a reputation to think of."

"Your name's already on it. You announced it yourself at our press conference last month. Look, we only really need to decide on the ending. Everything else is determined by what the programmers want to put in the game."

"I think the ending should be unresolved. Great fiction trades in ambiguity and shadow."

"Yes," I said, "there's going to be a cliff-hanger to set up the sequel."

"No, not a fucking cliff-hanger. Don't you know the first fucking thing about serious writing? There needs to be a kind of half-broken epiphany. A last beautiful secret sound that you're not even sure you heard."

His most recent novel, I recalled, had been called *Warlock's Gauntlet*. "I don't think we can put either of those things in a computer game," I said.

"In that case I think it should end with the Dragon being made to clean the kitchen naked on all fours and then slurp water out of a fucking dog bowl because that's all the bitch is good for."

I didn't really know what to say to that.

By the end of the day, we had nothing down on paper. I went home to my damp flat and wondered what I was going to do. The next morning, he turned up with a bottle of supermarket own-brand bourbon. There were no clean glasses in the office kitchen and no ice tray in the freezer so he had to drink it lukewarm out of a promotional mug. I could tell he was eager, somehow, for me to notice that he was boozing; but often he seemed to forget about the mug, and he'd go a long time with taking a sip, then at last he'd remember again, and he'd rush over and take a gulp, trying to catch up with himself, turning away from me to hide the grimace on his face. By the end of the day, he was torpidly drunk, and he started telling me about all the unspeakable benders he went on, and the unspeakable hangovers that followed. In his tone of voice as he told these anecdotes, there was an almost canine desire for approval, and it reminded me of being a teenager, when at the beginning of the school term everyone would swap stories about what they claimed to have done over the holidays, always careful to balance excitement with plausibility.

Day after pointless day went by like this. The Dragon refused to accept any of my suggestions. The only endings he ever came up with himself involved humiliating sexual violence against the Dragon, who he always seemed to assume was female. Sometimes I reminded him that we were only supposed to have a week to finish, and he told me angrily that you should never meet deadlines "because then you lose their respect". There was something desiccating about the conference room's stale air and stale light, and I became convinced that my fingernails weren't growing any more.

One day, on a hunch, I got my boss' secretary to find out if the Dragon had ever been married. It turned out that he had, but his wife now had a different address. That evening I called her at home and explained that I was working with her husband.

"Right. What has that got to do with me?" In the background I could hear piano music, something sparse and difficult.

"He seems to have some… well, 'issues', an American might call it, with women."

"Yes. We are going through a very, very unpleasant divorce. He tells everyone I've bankrupted him. But I've hardly taken anything. Just my minimum share. After all, I was his maid and his typist and his editor most of the time he was writing all those books. The real reason he's broke is, the Inland Revenue asked him for eight years' unpaid taxes, and his publishers want the advance back for a trilogy he never bothered to start."

"Oh. We did wonder why he'd taken the job."

"How are you finding him? Delightful company?"

"Not quite. His drinking is a bit out of hand."

She laughed, and then told me that the Dragon had never had a real drink problem. "He puts it on. He knows he's a boring man and he thinks a drink problem will make him more interesting. But it's got twice as bad since our separation."

"Why? Because he's upset?"

"No. I told you, he doesn't even like getting drunk that much. When he's upset, he just eats. But he wants to be able to tell people that I left him because of his alcoholism. It sounds tortured and important. He doesn't want anyone to know the real reason."

"What's that?"

"As I said: he's boring."

"So what can I do?"

"If you want him to cooperate?"

"Yes."

"Just play along," she said, and then hung up on me.

The next day, I waited until the Dragon went to the vending machine for a chocolate bar—he still never seemed to be able to make it work—and then positioned myself round the corner, out of sight but very much in earshot. I put my mobile phone to my ear. "Yeah, I'm just finding it really hard," I said loudly. "I've looked up to him ever since I was a child. He was like a god to me. Those books... And now I find out he's just a human being. A mortal, like the rest of us. He drinks and smokes and swears, and he has bad moods, and bad days. I mean, it's not that I blame him for all that. The life he's lead—he's obviously seen things the rest of us will never see. There's enough darkness and sorrow in him for three men. And it's not as if he can't take his booze like a Cossack. But still—I feel like Budd Schulberg meeting Scott Fitzgerald. So disenchanted. Like my world's been turned upside down. I'll never look at his books the same way again, now that I know the truth. They're not just the product of an extraordinary mind—they're the product of a scarred, stained, dented heart. All in all, I'd say that this week has been one of the defining experiences of my entire life. In forty years, when I'm giving his books to my grandchildren, I'll think of all this, but I won't bring it up, because I won't want them to know. For god's sake, never meet your heroes. Yeah. Yeah. I know. Thanks. Yeah. OK, bye."

I put my phone back in my pocket and walked back round the corner, then tried to look surprised when I saw The Dragon standing there. He looked back at me with moist eyes. Then he lumbered over and gave me a hug. "I know this week can't have been easy," he said, his mouth disconcertingly close to my ear. "I know I wasn't what you were expecting. But it's a lesson we all have to learn."

"I don't know what you mean," I said, as if I were desperate to admit he was right.

He released me. "What's the latest ending?" he said.

"The Dragon has the player trapped. They fight for days, but neither can get the upper hand. Then, finally, the player tricks the Dragon into thinking he's joined the Dragon's cult. The Dragon accepts his tribute, and just then, when the Dragon drops his guard, the player escapes the cave, and the cave collapses on top of the Dragon."

"That sounds good enough."

"You're happy with that? I can give it to my boss and you'll actually put your name on it?"

"Yes. So the Dragon dies at the end?"

"Not necessarily. We have to leave it open, like I said. They might want to bring the Dragon back for a sequel."

"Hope they don't. I hate fucking cash-ins. I'll probably get roped in again."

"Yes," I said. "I hope they don't, too."

The following year, the Dragon published another novel. His publisher sent us a copy, and I thought I might as well try to read it. Most of the book was taken up with a long, mawkish and incoherent dialogue between an ageing wizard and his worshipful apprentice. Then the apprentice, newly emboldened, goes off to rape and kill the mad ice witch on a dragon steed who once crippled his master. That scene went on for nineteen unbelievably graphic pages. I dropped the book off at a charity shop on my way to work.

The year after that, our company started work on *Dragonblade 2*. We didn't ask the Dragon back, because market research about the previous game had shown that attaching even quite a prestigious author's name to the game had only a marginal impact on sales. After all, most of our players didn't read.

And the year after that, I got a call from the Dragon. He was on a tight schedule with his latest novel, he said, and his publisher had suggested that he employ a freelance ghostwriter. Would I be interested? He couldn't pay much, but I could stay in his house—he had a new girlfriend from Poland who was a good cook. I was honoured by the request, I said, but our week together on *Dragonblade* had taught me that it was best to keep a bit of distance from your idols. He was disappointed, he said, but there were no hard feelings. He quite understood.

Illustrated by Hannah Waldron

WHY ARE
YOU AWAKE?

Written by Evie Wyld

I've been awake all night. My nose won't stop running because I drank too much beer in the evening when what I wanted was a glass of water. I've taken my place at the kitchen window where I can look out at the rest of the street, which is a soft grey. The street lamps are still on and a few early morning taxis are arriving, taking people to train stations, airports. I'm hoping that he won't be able to sleep without me there and he'll come and take me back to bed. I see the stray black dog is taking himself for a walk early today. Once I saw him piss on the people opposite's milk bottles. It was a great joke.

Why are you awake? Is the question he usually asks when I get up in the middle of the night and sit at the window. It's a rhetorical question, but I still try and answer it. The most truthful one is *Because I couldn't sleep.* But sometimes, to keep him awake longer, and with me, I make up a dream, something odd enough to sound genuine—*my thumbs were on fire, I was you but really you were someone else entirely.*

One of the reasons I got up was to let him sleep; I was messing around, blowing my nose, draining the last of the water on the nightstand. Sometimes when I get like that he'll get annoyed and call me a fidget, his way of saying *can you please stop that?* Other times he just puts an arm over me and tries to hold me still in his half sleep. I got up so that he could sleep, but I'm hoping he can't. I'm bad at laying in. I only like bed at bedtime, all other times it's a cheap trick.

One time I masturbated when I thought he was asleep, but he wasn't. How I knew he wasn't was, when I'd finished, he put his arm over me and faked a little snoring. I keep hoping to catch him at it, to even things up, but so far he just sleeps softly.

A fox is standing still in the middle of the road, as my neighbour drags her defunct television to the people opposite's skip. She gets it there, with a lot of trouble, and I wonder if her partner is asleep too, if this is what she does when she can't sleep—gets rid of the heavy objects in her house. The fox skitters away with more important things to worry about. The television is too heavy to heave into the skip, and so my neighbour leaves it on the pavement close by, and walks back briskly to her front door, her hands warming under her armpits. The black dog bumbles back up the road and only raises his ears slightly at my neighbour. He has done far worse to the people opposite.

Illustrated by Adrian Johnson

Written by Richard Milward

EPISODE I

The work was mindless, and the pay was shite, but at least it involved getting his hands wet. Just as the diners liked a good burp after munching on their £18.95 steaks, the sink liked a good burp after Daniel had finished the dishes. He watched the mucky foam swirl down the plughole, matted with crumbs of food, like an old bloke's beard. Then, Daniel washed his hands again, for good measure—this time without Fairy—and rub-a-dub-dubbed them dry on his jazzy apron.

Daniel couldn't wait to get home and wash his hands again, properly, with the aloe vera Carex. He'd considered bringing the Carex into work with him, but the trouble with folks with OCD is they hate the idea of other folks finding out about it. Raised eyebrows! Curses! Hellfire!

Daniel untied his apron, and hung it back on the peg he liked. He wasn't in the mood to find any of his workmates to say "Bye" to, especially not the female supervisor he liked. He used his elbows to open the back door to the kitchens, then followed the path around the side of the hotel, with his hands in his pockets. His heart dropped when he realised there was a bit of foreign fluff in his left pocket, and that he'd already touched it with bare fingers.

Twenty minutes later, Daniel was charging up the clean-smelling corridors of his building. Daniel lived alone in a brand-new apartment on the outskirts of town, not that far from the old Shell garage. He couldn't resist the apartment's untouched bathroom and freshly-laid beige carpets, and he was willing to pay £505 a month for it, despite only earning the paltry dish monkey wage. He was already behind on last month's rent and, sadly, Mammy and Daddy refused to bail him out this time, because they're getting the new conservatory put in, and because Daniel's twenty-eight years old.

However, for the time being, the rent was the least of Daniel's worries. There was the small matter of foreign fluff to sort out first. Daniel grudgingly had to touch his keys to unlock his front door (he tried it with his elbows once, but Chris from number 14 caught him in the act, and definitely frowned), then shouldered it open, kicked off his shoes, and ran up to his bathroom.

To Daniel, the squeaky bathroom door was a familiar, comforting sound that heralded the temporary suspension of purgatory. To his neighbours, it was a pain in the arse. At times, his neighbours had considered posting him a can of WD40 for the hinges but, like Daniel, they too didn't want to be seen as strange. And, for all they knew, it might not even be the squeaking of an ungreased door—it could be the squeaking of his bedsprings during regular, rampant masturbation. After all, the squeaking was always closely followed by Daniel's taps going on and off, and the odd grunt.

Daniel let out a satisfied breath, as he cleansed his paws under the hot tap. He foamed them up with two squirts of aloe vera, then rinsed, then dried. The towel was already beginning to smell damp, he reckoned, so he untucked it from the radiator, and swapped it for one of seven matching handtowels in his airing cupboard. The boiler gurgled, filling up again, ignoring Daniel painstakingly realigning the other six. Wonky handtowels! Bad housekeeping! Hellfire!

After averting all that hellfire, Daniel was in the mood for a cup of tea. He plodded back down the stairs, adjusted his lampshade, readjusted it, then went through to the kitchen. He filled up the kettle, rewashed the teaspoon he'd washed that morning, and couldn't resist rewashing his hands, for good luck.

While the kettle heated up, Daniel went back through to the hallway, to sort out the post. On the off chance the envelopes weren't self-stick, Daniel sliced open the letters with his penknife. He couldn't stand the thought of his finger sliding across some stranger's sticky spittle, though he did quite like the idea of having an excuse to wash his hands again.

The first letter had a logo at the top: NORTHUMBRIAN WATER. In the kitchen, the kettle clicked itself off, as Daniel flicked his eyes across the text. His mouth became suddenly dry. A mixture of anger, panic, and eternal damnation loomed in Daniel's skull. By the looks of it, Daniel hadn't been keeping up with his water payments. By the looks of it, the board would be shutting off his water before the end of the week.

EPISODE 2

If only there was someone around to see it, Daniel would've thrown a wobbly. However, when you live on your own, the only way to react to bad news is to sit down and wallow in shut-lipped anguish. The cup of tea didn't help. Daniel wanted to scream, but his walls were thin and he knew his neighbours were already back from work.

Daniel felt twice as hot as he did before he'd opened the letter. He wanted to strip off and cleanse himself properly in the shower, with the Radox Nourish shower cream, but the thought of it being his last ever wash made the back of his throat itch.

While the clock ticked and tutted at him from across the room, Daniel was seriously considering phoning home. The idea of moving back in with his parents made him squirm, but so too did staying in the "bachelor pad" with no water. What if the one he liked at work accidentally invited herself round one night? He wouldn't be able to touch her without knowing his taps were definitely working. AIDS! Fanny batter! Hellfire!

There was only one thing for it: Daniel decided to run a bath. He collected the metal sieve from above the sink, and the metre-stick from his cupboard of odds-and-sods. While Daniel preferred showering to soaking in salty homo sapien soup, he had to be conservative about the contents of his hot water tank. He squirted a liberal amount of Milk & Honey Radox into the tiny, steamy Niagara, then dipped the metre-stick into the tub, holding it as steady and vertical as possible. The tub was 47CM deep.

Daniel span the taps off the moment the water hit the 32.9CM mark. Daniel loved symmetry. Humans are almost made up of the same proportion of water as the planet they live on: 70-ish percent. Therefore, the bathtub had to be 70 percent full, too.

Daniel placed the sieve within reach of the tub, then lowered himself gingerly into it. He felt instant relief. He was going to stay in the bath, until he figured out an answer to his predicament. He waited patiently for a message to emerge in the soapsuds, like reading white tea leaves.

Nothing came. For the next couple of hours though, Daniel was content. He managed to keep the bath at a decent temperature, letting a few centimetres swirl down the plughole before topping it back up to 32.9CM with more hot.

He used his toes to turn the tap—under no circumstances were his hands getting involved with the mould reproducing on the fittings.

Soon enough, Daniel looked like a prune. His flesh was softening with every passing minute—now and then, he used the sieve to catch floating flakes of his dead matter, and tipped them out onto the lino. Osmosis was increasing his body water content to that of a cucumber, or a pint of lager: almost 90 percent.

He was drunk on bubble bath, but no closer to that all-important epiphany. The more he tried to focus his mind, the more elusive the answer seemed to get, like fishing for an invisible minnow. Aside from deep-sea diver or lifeguard, he couldn't think of any wet jobs like the dish monkey-ing—and Daniel couldn't swim. Perhaps the answer was just to dissolve completely, and disappear down the plughole, tax-free. The outside world did seem less and less appealing, the more the hours ticked by. Daniel wanted to cry, but he didn't want to disrupt the proportion of water-to-bathtub. Asymmetry! The bathtime bends! Hell! Hell! Hell!

Before long, his hands looked elderly: white, wrinkled and swollen. He tugged on the plug to let a little more water out, but even that tiny exercise was strenuous now. It was as if all his movements were in slow motion—waterlogged, heavy and lumbersome. He went to twist the tap with his toe, but couldn't find his right or left foot in the froth. Daniel hissed. He tried again. His bottom lip started to tremble, as he realised what the problem was.

He couldn't move his legs.

A mixture of osmosis and deep vein thrombosis had anchored Daniel's thighs and calves to the bottom of the bathtub. Through the water, they looked like blue-grey logs. Panicking, he tried to shift himself, but could only flap half-heartedly, making baby waves.

In the next room, Daniel heard his phone vibrate, politely asking to have its battery recharged. Simultaneously, Daniel's belly rumbled. And the bathroom light bulb sputtered out.

Trying not to lose his marbles, Daniel guessed the first line of action was to sort out the ratio of water to bathtub. As it stood, the tub was only 63.2 percent full.

Grudgingly, Daniel got his granny-fingers round the mouldy hot tap, and span it anti-clockwise. The tap dribbled slightly, then sneezed. Daniel span the tap further. The tap coughed out thin air. It was only when Daniel had spun the tap completely anti-clockwise—and almost out of its socket, he was that frantic—he realised the water board had already cut him off.

EPISODE 3

Daniel could feel his lungs seizing up, as he swam through crystalline water with a thousand streamlined polar bears. One by one, the polar bears turned pink, then red.

Suddenly, one of the polar bears swiped him across the face. Spluttering, Daniel woke up. He coughed a waterfall of phlegm out of his lung cavities. It was the thirteenth time he'd nearly died from drowning/exhaustion/hypothermia.

Daniel still couldn't move his legs. It'd been almost a fortnight since he'd run the bath—Daniel's skin was now flapping around his bones, and coloured yellow. It could've been jaundice, or it could've been that he'd resorted to pissing in the bath. Roundabout, frozen stools circumnavigated him in the foamless, grey murk. The water was icy—while his flesh had fallen away from his skeleton, Daniel's organs had shrivelled up tight and retreated into his ribcage, like unhappy campers in the Arctic.

Since his neighbours were polite people, no one had disturbed him over the course of the fortnight. Weren't they worried his bathroom door had stopped squeaking? Maybe they thought he'd finally splashed out on WD40.

In the darkness of the bathroom, Daniel had quickly lost track of what was night and what was day. Knowing his luck, on the odd occasions he found the strength to scream "Help!", it was probably between 9AM–5PM on a weekday, and everyone within earshot was at work.

If it was any consolation, Daniel had got over his OCD. Waking up to find one of your own stools bobbing against your bottom lip does put your quirks into perspective. Daniel sighed, holding back the sobs. Again, he tried to lever himself out of the bath with both hands, but not even the muscles cultivated from dish monkeying could carry the weight of his swollen legs and torso. He was imprisoned in tap water.

Daniel resorted himself to the fact he was probably going to die in the bath. The only thing for it was to force another sleep. However, there was no fooling Daniel's subconscious—knowing this might well be his final sleep, Daniel found it harder than ever to drop off. He even started counting sheep, but suicide-by-sheep-counting didn't seem the most heroic way to bow out.

Half an hour later, Daniel was humming a lullaby halfheartedly, when there was a knock on his front door. He shifted in the bath, getting a pang of icy excitement.

"Help!" Daniel whined, as loudly as his lungs allowed. He wished he hadn't worn down his vocal cords on the lullaby now. The cry sounded tinny in the tiled bathroom—he doubted even the silverfish could hear it, under the tub.

"Hello?! Daniel?!" yelled a deep male voice, from the corridor. Daniel didn't recognise the voice—then again, he didn't even recognise his own fingers any more.

"Help!" Daniel whined again. He chucked the metal sieve limp-wristy against the bathroom door, in desperation.

"Daniel?! Is that you?!" yelled the overfriendly stranger.

Daniel blinked, seeing pink polar bears again. Was this Heaven? Or was it just one of your run-of-the-mill, mortal guardian angels, coming to save him?

"Help!" he repeated.

"That's him, that's him," said a younger, female voice.

"We're coming in!" the deep voice shouted. After a couple more knocks, there was an almighty, deafening bang on his front door. Fortuitously, his guardian angels had come equipped with a battering ram. Even handier, the brand-new hinges didn't put up a fight.

By the sounds of it, the door smashed open in one go. The intense crackle-crash was followed by heavy, regulation booted footsteps. Daniel didn't care if they trudged mud into his freshly laid carpet—if he got out of the bath alive, he was going to wear shoes in the house from now on, too.

Daniel had managed to raise a slight smile, by the time the two police officers barged in to save him. Heavenly light poured in. However, Daniel's smile quickly faded, when he saw who was standing behind the officers: his supervisor. Of all the supervisors in all the semi-well-known hotel chains in the area, it was the female one he liked.

Both the female and the policemen spluttered, horrified, staring at scrawny Daniel soaking in his own sweat and shit. Daniel hung his head, as the female one retreated back into his bedroom, where—it's worth mentioning—Daniel had forgotten to hide his girly manicure and pedicure kits.

He felt like a fool, as the beefy policemen hauled him out of the bathtub, with rubber-gloved hands. A nugget of faeces clung to Daniel's shin-hair, as he rose from the froth like a scraggly rag doll. He coughed out another lungful of bathwater.

In the other room, Daniel could see the female one staring fixedly at his carpet. He wanted to mention, "It's new, that carpet; brand new," but the chance of them ever getting hitched looked unlikely now. In the past, Daniel often fantasised about the first time she'd see him naked—he never once imagined he'd have his own shit stuck to him, and the body of an eighty-year-old.

All things considered, it was probably time for Daniel to get a new job. That was the answer. After all, he now had two month's rent, as well as that blasted water bill, to pay off—and he needed a new, nubile supervisor to lust after, and not talk to.

First things first, though. As Daniel lay face-down in a pile of his own mushy skin-flakes, he knew what he needed most of all was a good, long wash.

Illustrated by Carson Ellis

Матрушка

Written by Tess Lynch

Victor and Elaine stepped out of the taxi on 9th Street, the morning light glittering off the windows of the brownstones. Victor heaved their luggage out of the trunk and paid the cab driver.

The honeymoon had been mostly pleasant, at times exquisite: Victor's aunt Anna had taken them to a performance of *Don Quixote* at the Bolshoi; they had heaped caviar on blinis and drank too much vodka in the Red Square; one night they bought two pills of what they were told was ecstasy from a teenager outside of a night club and stayed up until dawn running their hands over the cool cotton sheets and talking. They made love on the balcony until paranoia set in, creeping thoughts of a grey soviet cell and stern foreign police, and then moved to a velvet chaise at the foot of the bed. There were errant moments of tension, of course— as Victor crossed the street, narrowly dodging zooming cars and leaving Elaine helplessly stranded on the other side, or when Elaine had too much to drink and had confessed to her husband that, though she felt she knew him better than anyone, he sometimes seemed to her to be a stranger, his heart packed full of nefarious secrets. The moments glowed with an eerie, ominous light, as if no longer just arguments between a pair of individuals but important signifiers of what would become a dreadful, bleak union. And then the tension would dissipate, creeping back into the shadows. Victor handed Elaine a cup of black, hot coffee. Elaine placed a tentative hand on Victor's shoulder. By the time they left the hotel room, they were gluing their palms together as they stepped into the Metro. And now they were home.

They dragged the suitcases up the building's front steps and the two flights of carpeted stairs to their apartment. Particles of dust swirled lazily in a cube of sunlight and the air smelled like tap water. Victor unloaded his belongings by the door and disappeared into the kitchen for a beer.

"It's not even noon yet," called Elaine from the living room. Victor grunted. He hadn't been able to sleep on the plane, staring out the window or at his reflection on its surface. "I think I'm going to take a shower," she said, digging through her suitcase for her toiletry bag. In a corner of the case was a balled-up sweatshirt of Victor's. "This is yours," said Elaine, though she knew that Victor couldn't hear her as he ran the kitchen tap to clear the rust. She tossed the sweatshirt on a sofa, where it unrolled and revealed an object the shape of a bowling pin, but about half the size. She left her suitcase open and picked up the object. It was a nesting doll with an almost mirror-like gloss, a thick clear lacquer protecting its bright paint. A small fat face, an old woman's, had been painted on the doll's head, and it was wearing a colourful painted cloak. Elaine tried to unscrew the top half of the doll. It was stuck. She felt an unpleasant and inappropriately intense sense of frustration, as though she could smash the doll to pieces. She remembered a drunken night in college, an hour spent trying to open a new jar of jam to spread it on some toast: she had hurled the jar against the wall, where it had not only shattered but dislodged a chunk of plaster that she'd paid for out of her security deposit. She had wept impotently on the floor, covered in glass and jam, as the bread burned under the broiler. Now the doll was smeared with prints from her sweaty palm and her heart raced.

"Victor," said Elaine as she stalked into the kitchen, "What is this?"

Victor was drying his hands on a dishtowel. He looked at

Elaine, saw the colour in her cheeks and the set of her jaw. "That's a doll," he explained. "So what?"

Elaine pointed the doll's head at Victor. "Open it," she demanded. "I can't open the damn thing."

"All right," said Victor carefully. "I didn't know that me having it would offend you." He gripped the doll's head and attempted to turn it. He gritted his teeth. He leaned into it. Elaine was staring at him. "This is really difficult." Victor cleaned his hands with a paper towel, swiping it between his fingers. He took a deep breath and tried again. The doll wouldn't unscrew. "Well, I give up." He put it on the counter next to the coffee pot.

"You can't give up. That's the point," said Elaine. "What's inside?"

"Smaller dolls," said Victor. "It's a nesting doll. It's just a regular nesting doll."

Elaine grabbed the dishtowel and flashed it under the tap. She gripped the doll with the wet rag and bent her knees as she tried to loosen the head. She shook her hands and tried again, her face slowly achieving a maroon hue. A small vein that Victor had never noticed appeared at her temple.

"Stop it before you blow your brain," advised Victor. "What are you hoping to find in there?"

"Where did you get it? Why didn't you tell me?" Elaine would not release the doll. Victor put his hand over hers to prevent it from turning. She swatted him away. "Stop! It's almost there!"

Victor backed away. "I found it sitting on a wall when I was getting a toothbrush," he mumbled. "Remember when I had to get you a toothbrush? You were taking a bath."

"But why didn't you mention it? Why wouldn't you show

it to me?" Elaine dropped the doll onto the linoleum, where it rolled to the baseboard by the trashcan. She collapsed into a chair by the breakfast table and began to cry.

"Fine," said Victor. He picked up the doll and stormed out of the room. When he returned, Elaine was staring out the window hopelessly. She saw the hammer in his hand.

"Don't smash it," she sniffled. "Don't ruin it."

"No, we have to know what's inside. It can't just be a bunch of dolls. It must be six waitress's phone numbers and a tiny stripper shrunk to the size of a thimble. It's probably my witness identification card, and you'll find out my real name."

"Victor, stop it," said Elaine in a tiny voice. Victor wrapped the doll in the dishtowel and sat it on the floor. He held it steady with one hand and raised the hammer. "Please," said Elaine. Victor brought the hammer down onto the doll, which flew out from under his hand and ricocheted against the cabinet that held the blender. Elaine shrieked. It rolled to a stop by her feet, and she picked it up and held it to her chest. "Don't touch it!" She screamed. Victor had gotten to his feet, the hammer hanging limply by his side. He looked at his wife: her tangled hair and puffy eyes, her quick breathing. He looked at the apartment door.

"I've got to get out of here," he said, and left still holding the hammer.

Elaine sat in the shifting light watching the shadows shimmering on the floor, the striated ghosts of tree branches and the lengthening angles of the bookshelf. She felt an immense calm and exhaustion now that she was alone, and she released her grip on the doll to stare at it thoughtfully. Its mouth was painted bright red and its eyes had little feathered crow's feet. She thought of Victor coming back from his walk and entering the Moscow hotel to show her the doll. *I found this on my walk,* he would have said, *how funny. Open it.* She would have unscrewed it easily to reveal a smaller doll, and then a still smaller doll, and at the very centre would have been an egg, perfectly round and cool. *Is it a pearl?* She would ask him.

She woke up in a puddle of drool, face-down on her crossed arms. The apartment was darkening, and Elaine realized that they hadn't turned the lights on when they'd come in. "Victor?" she called. There was no answer. Elaine stood up and glanced around the living room—Victor's reading chair and his stack of old plays, the vase she'd bought before they were married, the television set and the two indentations on the sofa before it. She changed into her underwear and got into bed. There was a noise, and she called out Victor's name again before realizing that it was just the upstairs neighbour. Her stomach was sour and heavy.

She woke up much later when Victor came in, tossing off his jacket and lumbering into bed, his hair smelling faintly of cigarettes. She didn't look at the clock. She flung an arm over him, which he accepted, and fell back into unconsciousness.

When they woke up in the morning, Elaine saw that the doll had disappeared. Victor brought her a cup of coffee while she sat on the balcony, shaded by the magnolia tree. He sat across from her in silence reading the paper, and she looked out across the courtyard at the rows of windows embedded in the apartment buildings, the figures inside too far away to make out.

Illustrated by William Goldsmith

The Bellevue Dead

Written by Michael Crowe

Lance is oblivious of the enormous set of rules which he lives by. For example, after finishing a book he particularly enjoys he sniffs twice. The unknown glowing double nostril reviews are sometimes performed in connection with other things too (driving through four green traffic lights in a row, entering a well decorated room in a dream, noticing decent public sculpture roughly twice his height, finding coins) but most directly, the sniffing is tied to literature. Poor or average books receive no nasal action after the final word. The book is gently closed and Lance moves onward. Other examples of Lance's rules:

- While walking on sand he puts his hands in his pockets. If no pockets are available he'll imagine a headache, and will unthinkingly drift inland, to beach-free bits.
- While discussing anything electrical he'll use small left-handed hand gestures.
- Whenever checking the time, if it's exactly half past any hour, he'll glance over to his left and give whatever's over there some fairly decent consideration.
- Whenever it snows he listens (only) to Mahler's Fifth.
- His diary entries are all made up of either 878 words, 820 words, 454 words, 90 words, 12 words or 1 word.
- Whenever he's stuck in traffic for more than ten seconds he thinks of Miss Clark.

Miss Clark has looked truly beautiful for eleven minutes of her life. Six minutes in 1983, two minutes in 1990 and for three minutes three minutes ago. She and Lance will one day get together. He of course, thinks she looks beautiful all the time. When they do finally kiss they'll wonder why it took them so long. Lance will show her his diary with constant references to Miss Clark and Miss Clark will show Lance her diary with constant references to Lance. Miss Clark will show Lance her various sparkling new endings to well sniffed classic novels. Lance will show Miss Clark secret paintings of major moments from his life with titles such as:

Christmas in Hospital.
Miss Clark's First Day.
The Neighbour Sees Me When it Snows.
Applause Children Stood.
Broken Leg.

But that smitten sharing is a long way off. Miss Clark's most recent bout of beauty came from looking confident and worried about Lance's speech, which he has to give in thirty minutes. If you take half an hour to read the next sentence then immediately after we can head to assembly. Lance has no idea what to talk about.

"Children... Hello. Welcome... Goodness there are a lot of you! Right then... As some of you may know I will no longer be teaching Art. Not any more... That doesn't mean you have to stop asking me questions about painting noises or drawing invisible chickens or anything like that. I'm still happy to answer your questions. But as of today I am your new Headmaster. Traditionally we often give lengthy first speeches and bore you all senseless... Not that our last Headmaster was, er... But... Now, as it's the start of er... Children, I'm sorry, you deserve better! What can I talk to you about? What should I talk to you about? Maybe you should decide… Millions of years ago when I was your age I often wished that adults would listen to me. I wonder, you, what would you like me to talk about?"

Resorting to audience participation was a dicey, desperate move. Miss Clark squeezed her hands together. The precocious child Lance has randomly chosen is called Betsy. She happens to be a founding member of a group called The Bellevue Dead, and is also the host of her very own yearly awards. She looks up at Lance and blinks twice while thinking. She itches the top of her head and blinks again.

Betsy began her annual awards after watching a few minutes of the Oscars when she was six years old. She didn't know any of the people involved or what they really did (probably for the best), nevertheless she thought it was dazzlingly magical and wanted to recreate some of that magical dazz herself.

The first year was a humble affair, with only two winners, her favourite pencil (World's Best Pencil Award) and her neighbour's dog (World's Best Dog Award). The trophy in both cases was a single strawberry, which Betsy considered to be the best possible prize on any budget. The dog, Harold, ate his trophy immediately and seemed thrilled just to have been nominated, let alone to have won outright. The pencil drew a heart around its strawberry and wrote a short acceptance speech, saying it was, amongst other things, "Very proud. Thanks to the tree I came from, I couldn't have done it without you."

A few years later the edible red trophies remained the same, while the various award categories grew. At the time of writing the awards given once a year are:

Culture:

Best single sentence in a book award. Best worst opening line to a poem award. Best pause in a film (not necessarily long) award. Best moment to go to an ad break during a television show award. Tastiest looking meal in a film or television show award. Best sofa in a soap opera award. Most unexpected sound in a piece of music award.

Carefully packaged strawberries are anonymously sent to the winners with no explanatory note. If a winner is too hard to track down, or isn't a person, then Enid just eats or buries or slam dunks the strawberry on behalf of the winner.

The awards for friends (mostly members of The Bellevue Dead) involve a small ceremony in Ruffey Lake Park. Everybody brings a punnet of strawberries and the best are selected as trophies. The awards are:

Most entertaining lie award. Best text message award. Best socks award. Best gift (not necessarily a gift given to Betsy) award. Best weirdest anecdote award. Best obscene drawing of Nicholas Cage award. Best recommendation award. Best worst Christina Aguilera impression award. Best unintentionally funny remark award. Best shocking in a good way thing for that person to do award. Most unpunctual (normally the last award given) award.

Finally there are the personal awards. For each one Betsy awards herself a strawberry dipped in chocolate, sometimes with a squirt of cream too:

Best most embarrassing moment award. Best biggest regret award. Best worst excuse for lateness award. Best most ridiculous lie award. Best most preposterous reason for crying award. Best what was I thinking award. Etc.

Lance shoots a quick look at Miss Clark as Betsy continues to mull over her answer. He looks back at Betsy. She blinks for the fourth time, the fifth time, the sixth time. She says, "Hmm…"

The Bellevue Dead is a group which meets weekly to discuss topics they all know next to nothing about. Anybody can suggest a subject, and as long as nobody has any sort of credible knowledge on it, they can begin.

Previous topics include: Medieval breakfasts, The thoughts of animals when looking at aeroplanes, Beverly Hills Cop 3, Interspecies communication, The Bloop, Hiding in Kenya, Napoleon's hands.

The group's eight members take it in turn to look after a guinea pig called Charles. Charles is always present during the discussions and has therefore heard every word uttered by The Bellevue Dead. If Charles falls asleep during a discussion, the meeting is over. To date, that's only happened once, ten minutes into a discussion on mortgages. It's been agreed that when Charles dies, the group will disband. Meanwhile, if any other member of the group dies, they'll be replaced with Kirsten. Despite not being a member, Kirsten sometimes looks after Charles. Kirsten's home is paradise for him. A genuine heaven. Kirsten's been told she can join the group any time she wants to, but she says she'd rather just wait her turn. The Bellevue Dead nod.

The group's symbol, as designed by Betsy, is a simple green square.

Betsy ends the blinking pause.
She tells Lance what she would like him to talk about.
Miss Clark smiles.
Lance sniffs twice.
He smiles.
His whole body fills with flowers.
Trees.
Oranges and potatoes.
Bolognese and Crunchy Nut Cornflakes.
He talks for a while.
The children give a standing ovation.

Illustrated by Ian Dingman

JENNIFER LOVE HEWITT & THE DEMON OF CARLISLE CASTLE

Written by Kevin Fanning

Jennifer Love Hewitt walked quickly across the lawn of Carlisle Castle, silhouetted against the gray skies of Cumbria. She pulled her coat to her chin, cursing northern England and longing for L.A. She was only six weeks through the ten-week shoot for her upcoming feature film, *Garfield: A Tale of Two Kitties*. The production had been plagued by setbacks and disasters, and it was hard to tell if these were just the usual movie set mishaps, or perhaps something more sinister. In either case she was a professional, and she would get through it. She had just finished a particularly gruelling scene with Roger Rees, and wanted only to return to her trailer and collapse, but she arrived to find a Creaign Demon in the process of murdering her co-star, Breckin Meyer.

The Creaign was a terrible little creature, with the body of a small boy, long, crooked arms with hands that ended in black talons, no ears or nose whatsoever, and two large black eyes, like windows into the very bottom of the ocean. It was rarely seen near civilization; perhaps the movie set had been built too close to the woods. When seen from afar Creaign demons were often mistaken for lurikeen, but Jennifer Love Hewitt knew lurikeen, and while they might be trickster assholes, they weren't beings of pure evil who killed her co-stars and fed upon their souls.

It all happened in the span of a few moments. She entered her trailer and saw Breckin's body crumpled on the floor. The Creaign was hunched over him, coaxing the white smoke of Breckin's soul up over his tongue. Jennifer Love Hewitt's body tensed instinctively and that was all it took for the demon to feel her presence. It snarled, turned, and vanished through the wall, running back across the heath to the dark safety of the nearby forest. Without thinking, Jennifer Love Hewitt dove through the window and raced after it. If she could capture it in the next few minutes, she could bring Breckin back to life, and the movie would finish on schedule.

She chased the Creaign across the field but it was too far ahead—she watched as it leapt and dove gracefully into a patch of elder bushes and disappeared. There was no movement or sound whatsoever, save the wind soughing through the trees. She could sense no trace of the demon. She was running out of time.

She whispered the name of a fire ghost and a globe of blue, opalescent flame appeared in the palm of her hand. The air crackled and smelled intensely of burnt copper. She threw the fire into the bushes, and like lightning the flame dispersed into a thin line and sailed across the copse, through bush and tree and rock, until at last it drew itself into a circle around the spot where the Creaign was hidden.

Jennifer Love Hewitt walked through the circle of flame and bent to look the creature in the eyes. It stared at her with a mixture of anger and fear, its eyes speckled with tiny dots of white, as though reflecting the universe. It was saying something, the words coarse on its papery tongue. It spoke a language far older than any she knew. What was it trying to tell her? An explanation? A plea for its life? A warning? Or perhaps an incantation of some kind, a curse. No matter. In the blink of an eye her hands were around its neck. It scrabbled frantically, but Jennifer Love Hewitt was still, and patient, and hardly noticed the scratches it managed to make on her arms and face before its body went limp.

She dragged the Creaign behind her as she walked back across the heath to her trailer. Along the way, she startled a murder of crows hidden in the rushes. They launched up into the ashen sky and circled each other wildly, screaming her name as she passed beneath them: *Love, Love, Love.*

Illustrated by Tom Gauld

Written by Craig Taylor

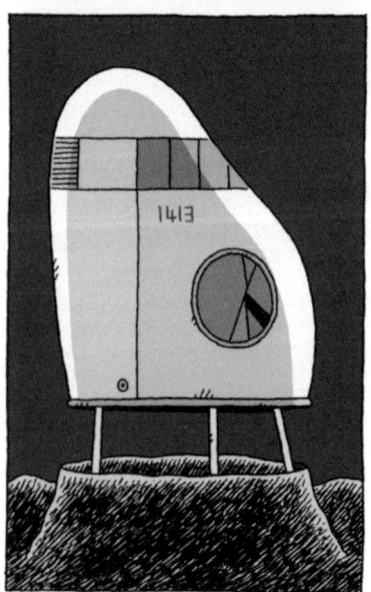

One evening, after he was questioned for two hours, the man was dropped off close to the apartment building. He took off his light tan coat and walked the final two blocks in his shirtsleeves. He thought of walking further, past his apartment, and maybe down the hill to Main Street, but in the still evening air he heard his metal bracelet hum and transmit his whereabouts. The humming only stopped when he walked up his apartment steps.

The next evening, after four hours of questioning, the man sat on the concrete steps in front of the apartment building in his shirtsleeves and watched the harvest moon above. It was then he felt the urge to describe to someone how the surface of the moon had felt beneath his boots. That conversation hadn't happened yet. During the questioning they never asked him about the moon, and he had no neighbours in the apartment block. The windows were always dark. There was never anyone in the lobby. Surnames were affixed to the mailboxes, but half the names were Jones, more than half. There were a few Smiths and some of the mailboxes were empty, their doors had swung wide open. Up in front of him, the harvest moon shone through the branches of the cypress tree. When the man looked down he noticed an eyelash resting on his wrist, so he pressed his finger to it, held it on the tip, and examined it before letting it fall. He then lifted himself off the step and walked upstairs.

On the fifth day of questioning in the white, well-lit room, the voice from the speaker behind the man's head sounded accusatory. On the sixth day the voice was friendlier. The man never looked back at the speaker embedded in the wall behind him. He sat in the metal chair in the centre of the room and stared down at his white, canvas shoes or stared ahead at the only art in the room, a photograph of the night sky hung on the wall in front of his chair. There were pauses between questions. Some were long enough for him to look out and identify Andromeda.

- Why were you in c6? the voice asked. He had been asked this question in each of the previous sessions.
- I was in c6 to perform maintenance, the man replied.
- Clarify.
- I was testing the capability of the external telescope.
- Where was she at the time?
- She was in d8.
- Clarify, said the voice.
- She was in the observatory.
- Her task?
- She was not assigned a task.
- Her reason? asked the voice.
- Personal, the man said.
- Clarify, said the voice, but the man stopped talking. He stared at the poster of the night sky. Almost forty minutes later the door slid open and he stood up slowly, as his left leg was asleep.

There were two on the mission. Each day, when she finished entering her data she withdrew to the observatory to sketch her impressions of earth. The first drawing she scanned in and sent back was the outline of a Christmas tree with a greeting to her parents written at the top. In the middle of the tree she drew the earth, a few clouds, the continents, and wrote below: Look up, way up. I can see your house from here.

It can be from both of us, she said to the man, quietly, in the part of the kitchen where the microphones couldn't pick up their voices.

- Clarify, said the voice the next day.
- I was in room c6, said the man. I was testing air filters and the remote capabilities of the telescope.
- Where was she at the time?
- The observatory.
- Please give the official name, the voice said.
- D8.
- Her reason?
- Personal time, he said.
- Clarify, the voice said, but the man did not reply.
- And when were you alerted to the presence of a foreign body in the observatory? asked the voice.
- I was alerted at 21:37.
- Clarify.
- I was alerted to a Code 723 at exactly 21:37.
- You left to investigate at what time? asked the voice.
- 21:40.
- Three minutes had elapsed.
- Yes, because the system had made previous errors. False alarms. The system, for instance, once identified objects in the greenhouse as foreign bodies, and by that I mean tomato plants. I didn't think this was an emergency, the man said.
- What did you find in the observatory? the voice asked.
- I'd refer you to my report, he replied.
- Clarify.
- There are full biological details in my report, said the man.

- Repeat the approximate diameter of the foreign body.
  The man crossed his arms.
- The diameter of the foreign body was approximately 11cm,
  he said.
- How did you dispose of the spore? the voice asked.
- In accordance to protocol, the man said.
- Estimate exposure time.
  The man said nothing.
- Estimate the amount of time the astronaut *Karen Ellen
  Thompson* was exposed to the foreign body. A different voice
  was used for the woman's name. It was louder and even less
  human; the two voices didn't match.
- *Karen Ellen Thompson*, the second voice said again into the
  white room.
- As per my report, the man replied, there was approximately
  seven minutes of exposure until the spore was identified and
  isolated.

When she was worried, Karen knotted her black hair into a
bun. When her data made no sense, or when she was frustrated, or when the slides cracked, even back down at home,
when her parents made her angry, when she was frustrated
by the secrecy in her life, she twisted her long black hair,
let it fall, twisted it up again. When the man had proposed
renting a motel room under a false name she twisted her hair
up, let it fall. Why don't we tell them all? she asked the man.
Tell them. I don't want this secrecy. During those moments
she stared straight at him, squared and defiant.

The motel was two hours outside town. The sheets were
shiny, the television crackled, the walls were thin but the

two of them could lie together all night. She ordered and then retrieved a pizza. Her civilian clothes were scattered in fragrant piles. After the pizza mission, they didn't leave. This can't be the first time this has happened, Karen said. Put people in high pressure situations and you get attraction. You've seen *Speed*, right? she asked, while brushing her teeth and leaning in the door frame.

This is not like *Speed*, the man said.

There are elements of it being *Speed*, she replied.

Do you think someone followed us? she asked as she tiptoed across the room. Do you think the room is bugged?

She picked up one of the dusty bedside lamps and said into the lampshade, Hello, Mission Control. We've got a naked astronaut here eating pepperoni pizza.

With the lights out, just before they fell asleep, she said to him: Definitely chicken nuggets. He said Roast chicken, at least the first time, with roast potatoes and roast parsnips, and nothing dehydrated, nothing out of a tube. That's what I'd choose. The second meal would be sushi.

I'm sticking with chicken nuggets, she said before kissing his neck. I bet they'll taste amazing.

Which dipping sauce? he asked.

No dipping sauce, she replied.

- Clarify, said the voice in the white room.
- Clarify what?
- Describe the symptoms, the voice said on the seventh day of questioning.

The man stared at the white walls around him. They seemed

to be lit from within.

- I refer back to my report, he said.
- Describe the rash.
- The rash was a patch of irritated skin on her torso that appeared immediately after exposure, probably in minute eight.
- Clarify, said the voice.
- The rash formed on her neck, clavicle, sternum, her breasts.
- Both breasts? asked the voice.
- Yes, he said. The voice went silent.

He had acted quickly. He brought Karen into the med chamber and examined her in his safety suit, touching her face with his gloves. Her skin had already drained of all colour. She was, at first, pale and then a few seconds later not just pale but chalky in spots, only red when he pressed his gloved finger to her lips, and only pale rose-red for a moment.

Hold steady, he said when he saw the rash was on her shins and moving quickly, prickling her skin. Patches of white formed on her toes. This is nothing, nothing, he said.

Tick the box, she said in a weak voice when she tried to lift herself. The box was the daily health report, beamed back down to earth.

We'll tick that box when we get to it, he said, I just need to do something. I need to solve this. When she looked at him he saw her white lips curve in an attempted smile. There was suddenly white spreading up from the roots of her hair.

I know what this is, I know how to handle this, Karen, he said. I know this. I know what this is. She knotted her hair up into a bun and let it fall and knotted it again and said I think we need help, and he said No we don't.

- Clarify, said the voice in the white room.
  The man looked straight ahead.
- I said to her you have to trust me because I wanted her to trust me.
- What else did you say?
- Words of comfort, the man replied.
- Clarify.
- I told her she was loved.
- Why was a health report not sent immediately?
- Because by 22:13, as per my report, I truly believed she was improving.

Her seizure was brief but by the time it passed her skin was white, her hair mostly white. She stopped shaking, and in that pause he watched the colour drain, from root to tip. He broke the seal and opened the orange box and rummaged past the pre-loaded syringes. Karen's breathing was little more than a rasp.

They spent Sunday in the motel. When they left, they sat in the car and he held her hand and he said to her, I value secrecy.

You think I don't? she replied. You think that's not an issue for me.

And you can ask me about them, he said. It's a bit strange you've never said anything.

I don't want to know, she replied, and put her sunglasses on. I don't want to know their names. I don't want to know if you have another child. I don't want to be told to stay silent. Then she started the car. The man thought it was important to mention secrecy once more but she leaned over and turned up the radio.

She had a second seizure. He didn't look into her eyes as he strapped her onto the examination table in the med chamber. She was hissing now, slapping her palms against the glass of his helmet. He clicked and fastened her in and finally looked at her collapsing face, her pupils now ivory white. She looked puzzled. Her mouth opened and another sound emerged. While she was chewing at the air a tooth lifted from her mouth out into the weightlessness of the cabin and began a slow rotation in the space. He followed it. She watched. Her eyes were bone white, more white than that.

- Clarify, said the voice.
  The man shifted in the chair.
- I left the med chamber for approximately two minutes, he said. The sedatives were in the sleeping chamber, B5.
- And on your return?
- As per my report…
- Clarify, the voice said.
- As per my report, the straps holding her, Thompson, had been cut.
- Cut or torn?
- The straps appeared to be severed.
- Approximately how much blood did you notice in the chamber upon your return?
- As per the photograph in my report…
- Answer, said the voice.
- A minimal amount. Droplets, the man said, and he saw them hovering in the weightlessness and the ripped straps waving in the air, like seaweed underwater. He turned and looked at the empty passage behind him. He searched the ship.
- Where is the body? the voice asked.

- I do not know, he said. Each day they asked him this question. Each day he replied the same way. The body disappeared.
- One final question for day seven, the voice said. How could the spore GBT-19 have been introduced into the observatory? How could *Karen Ellen Thompson* have been exposed? Again, her name was spoken in a different voice.
- As per my report, the man said, there are multiple explanations. I have answered this question every time I have taken this seat. Without fail, I have answered this question…
- Thank you, the voice said.

A car dropped the man off in front of the apartment building. Again the man tried to walk down the hill to Main St and again his bracelet began to hum. He returned to the apartment building. There were no lights on in any of the windows. There was no light on in the lobby and even the sodium light above the concrete steps was dark.

The man opened the door. He clicked the light switch but the room remained dark, so he felt the ridges of the mailboxes to guide him to the elevator. The elevator was dark so he walked up the stairs in the dim yellow of the emergency light.

He entered the apartment and found his flashlight in the closet. The chair was in its place and the television was in its place. He flicked the light switches. Nothing. He shone the flashlight and caught a glimpse of something on his tan coat. There was a hair on his coat. He picked it up between two fingers and examined the long black hair in the beam of light and then let it drop to the ground. He entered the bedroom and sat down on the bed and shone the flashlight on the other pillow which was usually plump but this evening was marked by a divot and in that divot rested another long black hair, which he pulled from the pillow case, examined in the beam of the light, and dropped to the floor. Then he heard a noise from the apartment upstairs. He heard footsteps. The man lowered himself onto the bed and pointed his flashlight up to illuminate the stucco dimples of the ceiling, like the surface of the moon. Again he heard the sound of slow footsteps crossing the room above. He clicked off the flashlight and quietly turned on his side as the footsteps continued. He looked at the cypress tree outside the window swaying in the autumn breeze. He slowed his breathing. He thought of Andromeda and then slipped his hand under the pillow, against the cool fabric, and touched the tooth waiting for him.

Stories → Illustrations

Written by Michael Crowe

Slow Brown Fireworks

Illustrated by William Goldsmith

I got a letter from an ex-girlfriend this morning. I've not seen her for something like ten years. Actually, since then I've moved house twice, god knows how she managed to get my address. Maybe through Alma or Howard. Probably Howard. 90% sure it was him. 10% Alma. He's very free with information. It's irritating when he's broadcasting about me, but it's tolerated because of all the tittle he tattles my way. Wave after wave of whispers. The contents of Alma's safe. Jean's eerie diary. Arthur's unravelling wickerwork webs. Sherry's fluorescent egg.

Howard often looks like he's about to be about to sneeze. It's almost almost adorable. There's spectacular video footage of him flying through the air with that look on his face, but we'll come back to that flying later. His parents (both recently deceased) educated him, purposely keeping him completely in the dark about various grand things, not in a nasty way, but so that the sense of wonder and magic about the world would remain with him throughout his adult life. On his eighteenth birthday Howard's parents finally told him about the sea, about giraffes, about chocolate and about music. Stood on a beach, staring out to sea with a mouthful of chocolate, headphones on, and an unseen giraffe approaching from behind. Now, years later, Howard wonders what else his parents had diligently worked to hold back.

For a while Howard was a teacher. Three dreams told him to start the class. He ignored the first dream. The second made him explode into action. The third was irritating, he'd already set everything up. For the first few weeks I was his only pupil. Excruciatingly embarrassing three hour lessons on things like, "Silences too far away to hear," and, "Birds' favourite architects." Bit by bit the class became popular. That's where I met my ex.

Howard talked to his students in a fake American accent. He told us it was fake. He was always upfront. The students respected that. The whiteboard would typically be full of compliments of the pupils at the start of the day. In addition to that, Howard thought nothing of handing out gifts at the start of each class. An apple still attached to its branch. Filter tips. A water damaged polygraph machine. A white shoe. An unnamed collie dog. Pebbles. Howard was fond of telling us to put our pens down, or to throw them at him. They'd bounce from his smiling face. He'd shout, "Good shot! Good shot! Close. Bit too high. Good shot!"

A typical Howard classroom speech,

"The carbon inside you was once inside a star billions of years ago. That star no longer exists, it exploded. Your carbon was blown out into the interstellar medium. It twirled and cycled around until eventually enough elements were whipped and pulled together to make another new star. This one also eventually exploded. The same process was repeated several times over millions of years. Eventually those bits ended up on Earth. Millions of years later through various biological processes, this carbon is now here as 18% of you. Therefore you're all stars, and you should twinkle and sparkle accordingly."

He encouraged us to get to know the classroom. To think about its emptiness when we got home. To massage our desks and tickle them underneath. To leave our shoes and socks overnight. To bring in knick-knacks, records, plants.

The initials of his last class topic were F.R. The students were to propose a topic with those initials. Whichever Howard liked best was going to be the focus of the class. He gave two examples: "Firing Rifles," and, "Future Regrets." Howard asked us to think of ideas and to watch quietly as he smoked his first ever cigarette. I thought fajitas reappear. I thought frog radar. I thought fast Rolex. I thought futon relaxation. I thought flung risotto. I thought fifty raccoons. I thought floodlit relatives. Howard stubbed out the cigarette. He stood up and told everyone that the class was cancelled. He told everyone it was his birthday. He asked if anyone would like to visit his parents with him. Everybody raised their hands. He said you won't all fit in my and was just about to say car when he burst into tears.

That was Howard's last class before becoming a stuntman. As I mentioned earlier, there is dramatic footage of him flying through the air. He enjoys the job as he gets to regularly have his whole life flash before him during frequent near death experiences. He told me that in these moments he sees everything with a weirdly glorious clarity. A layer of slime is wiped away and he sees his parents in spectacular detail. His mum's eyes as she turned to look at him and his dad's eyebrows when he was excited or in dire need of the toilet. He remembers hundreds of hours of conversation. He remembers every time he caught a ball, or sneezed, or laughed at something or felt stupid, or lonely, or bored, or thrilled, or ill. He remembers the yellow and pink carpet in his first bedroom. He remembers the weight of unwrapped gifts. He remembers the moments he fell in love. He remembers the faces of all the people he taught. He remembers the class-room door, the light switch. He remembers his last lesson and what his lovely students did after he stopped crying and told them that his parents had died. In the spectacular foot-age, as he flies along, he looks like a terrified Superman. The perfectly timed explosions and fireworks grow and burst all around him, the motorbike he was on spins far away, the size of a toy. The last time I visited him (in hospital) he told me that if he ever manages to watch the video he could pause the exact moment he was remembering a long forgot-ten dream in which he was told by a little yellow flower that the most important element was missing from everything. From every book, the most important paragraph was miss-ing, from every film the most important scene, from every conversation the most important sentence, from every meal the most important ingredient, from every room the most important item, from every etc. etc. etc. Then he told me that just before he landed, he knew that if he somehow mi-raculously survived, he would try to fill in some missing bits. I didn't know what to say. There was a hospital pause. Then he asked me if I'd brought the grapes he'd asked for.

Anyway, I should digress less. This morning, a letter from my ex-girlfriend arrived, shuffled in with assorted bills. She basi-cally just told me Howard is doing much better now (I know) and asked if I'll fill in a questionnaire which she's sent out to all of her ex-boyfriends. Nicely typed up and spaced out but judging by the questions, I think she's going through a dif-ficult patch. Not quite a mental breakdown, but something not too dissimilar. Maybe it is a mental breakdown, I don't know. It starts off reasonably sane, asking my age, my height, weight, that sort of thing. My middle name. All fine. Then:

Judge your overall sexual performance with me on a scale of one to one hundred.

I put a modest sixty-four. I toyed with an eighty something for a while, then wrote twelve, scribbled it out and wound up with the six and four. Next question:

Why do you think I never had an orgasm with you?
A: Inadequate size of penis.
B: Poor physical hygiene which turned me off completely.
C: Shoddy, slapdash, unskilled technique.
D: Your insistence on one preposterous position.
E: I never wanted to do it but I just felt so sorry for you.

I ticked them all. Then a few questions about how much I'm earning, if I have any children, and:

Who would you rather have your life saved by?
A: Batman.
B: Superman.
C: A Chinese Sherlock Holmes.
D: Spiderman.

Spiderman. Then there's an extremely long-winded section, with about thirty questions including:
- Have you ever thought about me while having sex with an-
other woman?

- Have you ever tried to recreate any moments we had with another woman?
- Is chilli con carne three times a week too much?
- How often do you think I think of you?
- Do you even remember the colour of my eyes?

I'd stopped answering the questions, I was just reading through to the end now. Then it does end, with this:

If we were to bump into each other again, where would you rather it be:

A: In a sauna.

B: On an oil rig.

C: In a morgue.

D: I love you.

E: Please don't think I'm mental.

F: I hand delivered this, I'm outside your house right now.

Written by Ned Beauman

XYLYL BROMIDE

Illustrated by Jim Tierney

In 1914, a few weeks before the war started, Barclay had met a fat man at dinner who said he always insisted his mistresses wear the same perfume as his wife. That way, he explained, he wasn't really being adulterous, because it made it impossible to think of them as distinct individuals—as far as his heart was concerned, they were just colonies of his beloved. Then, when they became too demanding, or he felt himself getting too attached, he would confiscate the previous perfume and instead prescribe them the one worn by his childhood nanny, whom he had found repellent. This made separation easy. In a way, Barclay blamed this man for what took place four years later, when his best friend Gerald Hayward was hanged for murder.

Barclay himself had never had a mistress, although he knew rumours had sometimes circulated that he was sleeping with Gerald's beautiful wife Sylvia while Gerald was away at the Front. He certainly wasn't, although he did go to the Hayward house in Kensington at least twice a week for tea. He'd known Sylvia since they were children, and as the war dragged on into the winter of 1917, she was more and more often in need of a reassuring presence. This was because of the disturbing letters she was getting from her husband. Gerald, a captain, very popular among his men, had been at Ypres when the Germans first used mustard gas. He had been lucky to escape with only mild blisters on his face and chest, and since then his division had come under gas shell bombardment at least a dozen more times. Gas, he wrote to her, was worse than anyone at home could imagine. It was like a biblical plague, he said, with all the men struck blind and butterflies falling out of the air. One day in December, Sylvia confided to Barclay that in some of Gerald's most recent letters, he wrote as if the horror of it all had driven him almost mad. There was so much talk at that time of shell shock.

Unfortunately, it was just then that the Foreign Office, Barclay's employers, asked him to go to Paris for a fortnight to take part in negotiations with the French Ministry of War. The last time he saw Sylvia before his departure, she told him she had a very silly request. When Gerald went to Paris before the war, she said, he had brought her back a wonderful perfume from a shop on Avenue Montaigne. She knew it was a waste to wear it when he wasn't there, but she did sometimes anyway, because it reminded her of him. By now, though, she had almost run out, and she so wanted to able to wear it for him when he was next back in London. Barclay told her that he'd be honoured to buy her another bottle. Privately, he suspected that if Gerald's mental condition didn't improve, he might have to come home sooner than Sylvia anticipated. The Germans were still using mustard gas relentlessly. That morning, he had read in the Times that they were now mixing it with xylyl bromide, a very potent tear gas with a deceptive odour.

As soon as Barclay got back from Paris, he took a taxi to the Hayward house with the bottle of perfume. Sylvia couldn't resist taking out the stopper for the first time in his presence. But when she sprayed a little on a handkerchief and sniffed it, she looked crestfallen. It wasn't quite the same, she said. It had a faint but unmistakeable smell of lilacs. Barclay explained that the perfumerie had been obliged to change the formula a little because of the difficulty of obtaining all the ingredients in wartime. And when you subtract one thing, they'd told him, you sometimes have to add two or three others to balance the fragrance. But they'd kept it as close to the original as they could. Sylvia said she was terribly grateful and she was sorry for seeming disappointed at first.

A few months later, Gerald was suspended indefinitely from command on grounds of nervous debilitation, and sent back to London. As the mustard gas bombardments went on, Barclay learned, he had withdrawn further and further into himself, until he was no longer capable of giving orders. Barclay called in a few favours with friends at the War Office to make sure that Gerald would be allowed to convalesce at home, with Sylvia, instead of at a military hospital. He decided to delay his own first visit to his friend until Sylvia could assure him that Gerald was doing better. Gerald wouldn't want Barclay to see him at his lowest.

Then one day in April, Gerald strangled Sylvia to death.

He was discovered by a maid trying to load a revolver, presumably so he could shoot himself, but his hands were shaking so hard that he kept dropping the bullets. A few feet away, Sylvia's body lay on the carpet. The maid gently took the gun from his hand, settled him in an armchair, and then called the police.

At the trial, his lawyer argued that a man undergoing treatment for terrible mental injuries received on the battlefield could not be held fully responsible for his actions, and indeed Gerald did not seem to be able to give any coherent explanation of what had happened. But the judge instructed the jury that there was no medical evidence that shell shock alone could disable a man's moral compass. At that stage of the war the attitude of the British public towards their armed forces was oddly intolerant, and Gerald was found guilty and sentenced to hang. The Hayward house was sold. Without Sylvia and without Gerald, Barclay was left very alone. He decided to find a wife. There was a great surplus of unmarried women in England, so he knew it wouldn't be any trouble.

On his wedding night, a month after Armistice Day, he presented his new wife with a bottle of perfume. She asked why it had already been opened, and he told her it was a very rare and expensive French scent that had once belonged to his aunt. Before her death, he claimed, he'd promised to pass it on to whomever he married.

The truth was he'd retrieved the bottle from the Hayward house shortly after Sylvia's murder. He'd told Gerald's lawyer that he needed to visit the house because there were some valuable old books there that he'd lent Gerald before the war, and he didn't want to lose them if Gerald were found guilty and the contents of the estate were auctioned. Gerald's lawyer clearly thought he was heartless for worrying about such a thing at such a time, but Barclay didn't care: he had to make sure the perfume wasn't found. There was hardly any chance that anyone would guess what he'd done, but he couldn't take the risk.

Despite what he'd told Sylvia, the perfumerie in Paris hadn't had any trouble with their formula. In fact, he'd had to pay them an extra hundred francs to add lilac oil to the perfume without changing the label on the bottle, which they were very reluctant to do. While Barclay waited for the mixture to be prepared, an earnest young apprentice had tried to make conversation with him. The apprentice said Barclay's order had reminded him of something he'd read in the newspaper that day about what the Germans were adding to mustard gas now. There was some new compound, he couldn't remember the name, but the newspaper said it smelt uncannily of lilac blossoms. It was so cruel, the apprentice said, to make men afraid of the scent of a flower. His customer had nodded but made no reply.

Barclay had never imagined that Gerald might murder Sylvia. The plan was just that he would leave her. He was supposed to come home and discover that his wife now evoked in him a horribly vivid memory of the mustard gas attacks that had driven him almost to catatonia. The real cause would never have occurred to him, because he would have been working all the time to sever his memories of war from his memories of home, and because the sense of smell was so hard to interrogate logically. Well, that much had worked. But after that, Gerald was supposed to find himself more and more alienated from Sylvia, until eventually he had no choice but to abandon his marriage, as that fat man at dinner had abandoned his mistresses. Sylvia would have divorced him, and four or five years later Barclay would have married her, as he'd planned to since he was thirteen. She belonged to him, he'd always thought, and it was only because of his timidity and bad luck that Gerald had got her instead. Gerald was his friend, but what use was he to her now that he was ruined by the war? That was how he had justified it to himself.

Now Barclay's new wife would sometimes catch him in the bathroom, standing shirtless at the sink, splashing his face and chest with scalding water from the hot tap, or in the pantry with a bottle of bleach, breathing in the fumes as deeply as he could bear. He got angry when she asked him what he was doing, and he also got angry whenever she came to bed without wearing the perfume. She couldn't have known, of course, that when he burned his skin or his lungs, he was trying to imagine what it had been like for Gerald; that when he drove himself savagely into her perfumed body, he was pretending he was dying, like a soldier, in an agony of lilacs.

"It had the faint but unmistakeable smell of lilacs"

Written by Craig Taylor

ASH BANDITRY

Illustrated by Tom Gauld

I. PLANE

- I would have expected more than a hug, he said.
- More? More would be physically difficult.
- But you could find a way.
- What, in all the turbulence? I asked.
  A shadow moved across the Flatmate's forehead.
- You could find a way, he said. If you knew it was going to be a fatal crash.
- When do you know that?
- Probably when you start plummeting. I would think.
  We both lifted our hands and made slicing gestures to dismiss the flight attendant's attempt to sell us duty free. I turned in my seat and looked out of the window at the brown and dusty patches of France far below.
- There would be a reflex in your mind, the Flatmate said, that would make you realize you're going to die.
- Something inside you? I asked
- Something in your primal brain that would force you to somehow get sex for the last time.
- Well, I'd give you a hug, I said.
- Yeah? OK. Thanks, he said and ripped a corner off the in-flight magazine and stared at his tray table. He ripped another strip. I wouldn't particularly want to end my entire life with a hug, he said to no one in particular.
- I'm not a woman though.
- That's how strong the urge is for me. And if it happens—he lowered his voice—all I'm saying is just slightly suck me off. If the plane's definitely going down.
- Why does it have to be me?
- Obviously I would reciprocate afterwards, the Flatmate said.

- What, during the tailspin?
- I'm conscious that you would also need to take care of the primal part of your mind.
- But you get to go first?
- God, Gerry, the Flatmate said. You put on your own mask before you put on the mask of the child.
- That's not a proverb, I replied. That's just an instruction.
- You can go first if we're on BA.
- Oh, right, ok. But on the cheap airlines…
- It's a fair system. It's a fair way to end.
- But you don't know until the end what is the actual end. The end end. And then I said quietly: What about her?

  The woman across the aisle turned the page of *Country Life* magazine.
- Oh, she'll be praying, the Flatmate said.
- And what if she looks over, you know, in the last few seconds of her life and sees two guys sucking each other off?
- Not at the same time, the Flatmate said. It's one at a time.
- So that's the image she takes with her, is it? Her prayer is interrupted.

  The Flatmate turned to look across the aisle. He had chosen to wear his suit again, the same mournful black with pant legs stained with mud from the cemetery. I had had mine dry-cleaned. There was a line of yellow on the collar of his shirt.
- I'm sure, the Flatmate whispered, that woman would get off one good prayer.

I had been thinking a lot about prayer in the last three weeks because it's a good way to fill the hours of a stress leave. I'd experimented a little with prayer but mine never fully left the room. They were too conversational: how are you? Do you miss, like, breakfasts?

I wouldn't even try one on a plane. Crash prayers would be a mess, all bruised from knocking against the plastic ceiling of the cabin and ricocheting in the space between the carry-ons. They'd finally get into the fresh air through the ripped fuselage and drift toward that faraway mail slot. Just ugly little parcels, especially on a budget airline, with all the do-overs and restarts and some people just repeating Oh God. Would that even count? That's what I didn't get with prayers. When do they go threadbare? When does God think, No, that's just a fucking noise? No.

- If you're worried about people watching, said the Flatmate, you could get an airline blanket.
- What, to put across? I asked him.
- Or to use as a curtain.
- No, they cost money. Everything costs money on this airline.
- You're lucky I'm choosing you.
- Oh yeah? You're just trying to make an arrangement.
- A reciprocal arrangement.
- I don't want my last experience to be with my head down there.
- If there's a crash. Only if. I don't want to do this either. In a perfect world I wouldn't have a guy sucking me off, especially you.
- I'm not going to.
- You think you're not going to.
- I'm not.
- What are you going to be doing?

The flatmate looked at me. Sometimes lately he'd look at me and say, we should put a tablespoon of him in the Seine. Or, we should put a tablespoon of him in the Mediterranean. His parents wanted one meaningful place. One scatter. We were trying to achieve a spread.

- I read somewhere, he said, that during a crisis a man and woman just look into each other's eyes and know they have to fuck before it all ends. So on some other flight, without you there, it could turn into full sex.

- You're not having full sex as a plane crashes.

- Well, you never know.

- Well, I do know.

- You've never been there.

- You don't understand the physics of it. There's physics involved. There's… physics.

The older woman stowed the *Country Life* magazine in her carry-on. The Flatmate placed a pound coin on the fold-down table.

- For the blanket, he said. Just in case. I don't mind paying.

He smiled.

We flew over a French lake with clouds resting on the surface, its water blue beyond blue. I only paid £4.99 to see that, I thought. Plus airport tax. I would miss the world, I thought. I would definitely miss the world.

- Why do you think he did it in France? I asked and the Flatmate exhaled. With it went the last mischief in his voice.

- Because it's the saddest country in the world.

I looked out of the window.

- Why do you think he did it in September? I asked. But the Flatmate was already ripping a strip off his in-flight magazine and looking the other way.

2. ROSENDER

The Flatmate stood at the far end of the garden with his head bowed and his hands clasped in front and it was only after a few moments I noticed he was rubbing his palms together. When he wandered back to the table he said, Smell this, and offered up the sprigs he'd collected in his cupped hands.

- I call it either Lavemary or Rosender, he said. It's a mix, of course, and I think, frankly, I'll sell it at the farmer's market.
- You're just rubbing your hands together.
- It's a technique, Gerry, he said. It's a French technique.

He walked back across the small walled garden. This was how the work divided. He rubbed wild lavender and rosemary into his hands and peered over the wall at the string beans growing in the neighbouring garden. I was in charge of securing the small, empty tubes of Kronenbourg before they gusted across the flagstones of this small house across from the abbey. We'd only landed four hours ago but the Flatmate drank in the cab from the airport. He masked the hiss of the tin by coughing loudly, though the old Frenchman at the wheel watched him in the rear-view.

- Rosender, he yelled from back amongst the bushes.
- I'd say it's more lavemary.
- I thought you'd say that. Would it say Lavemary on the cover of the expensive hand cream I'm going to make from this process? I think this hand cream would be called Accent Agout. Pour l'homme et…
- La femme.

- Et le cheval et le petit jambon. But that is it. That's it, Gerry, he yelled. Because it's exclusive.

Then came the sound of the cicadas. Then came the sound of a small, French motorcycle somewhere in the hills. He walked back with another handful and stood near me, crushing his palms together, forcing out air.

- To answer your question, he finally said, no.
- I don't remember the question.
- About love.
- From an hour ago?
- From right before I made my fragrance discovery.
- Right.
- The answer is no. I just haven't felt it, felt it all. I've been mouth in love though. You know, when you're just with someone because of the shape of their mouth?
- No, I don't really know that one.
  He looked up at the sky.
- I've been voice in love, I've been intelligence in love, I've been breasts in love, I've been sense of humour in love, I've been 'their family' in love, I've been sex in love, arse in love…
- That's surprising, I said. That's really surprising, that one.
- And I've been innocence in love, and I've been… what's the opposite of innocence these days?

The cicadas again.

- Worldliness, I guess, I said.
- Then I've been wordliness in love.
- Never a combo, I asked.

- Yes, sometimes a combination, he said. It's not like these
women are hideous goblins. Obviously, sometimes you get a
combination. Obviously.
- How many combinations do you need?
- How many combinations do you need? he replied.
- I need two.
- You don't really need two.
- Three and I would be ecstatic, absolutely ecstatic, and I'm
sure I would be just worshipful, just over the moon.
- Look what happens to melon rinds in the sun, the Flatm-
ate said.

The four slices on the table were dry and white and covered
in a light dusting of ash. The Flatmate picked up his waiting
cigarette and tapped the long curve of ash onto the melon
carcass, then pointed towards the wading pool in front of
us, in the middle of the courtyard. Water from the local
river was piped through and it rippled the surface and gently
shook the green algae on the bottom.

- Do you think they bathed him in there? the Flatmate asked.
As a child?
- They have a bathroom for that. It's a summer home. There's
running water. It's a not like a UN refugee tent.
- Maybe just to keep cool.
- I would think they'd use the river for that sort of thing.
- Hmmm, said the Flatmate. He wiped the remains of the
rosemary and lavender on his trousers. Do you think they
baptized him here?
- No, they're not Baptists, I said.
- What does that matter?

- They wouldn't do a full body immersion.
- Do you think he was baptized?
- I know he was. When they had all those photos laid out?
- Where?
- At the back of the reception. His mother showed me.
- How did his mother look in those photos from back then?
- I don't know.
- A little smokingly hot, I suppose.
- I wasn't really looking.
- Right, because you don't look at that kind of thing.
  And then the Flatmate asked, Are you baptized?
- Sure, I told him.
- So am I. It sounds like capsized a little, doesn't it?

He finished his cigarette by pressing it into the melon rind
and even though the skin was dry, a lip of melon juice rose
high enough to extinguish the burn. It stuck in.
- That's considered torture by some melon governments.
- So is watermelonboarding, I said.
- Yes. That's true. The Flatmate asked. Have you ever baptized
  a girl with come?
- No. I can honestly say that's not something I've even remo-
  tely done.
- Me neither. I don't even know how you'd do it, really. They
  usually use a whole pool, don't they?
  I exhaled.
- Well, I said, you couldn't have a full baptismal.
- I don't know if it would even be legit.
- It wouldn't be legit in the church.
- I know.
- And there's no use asking why…

- OK, all right, he said.
- Because, you know why.
- I know, I know. It's ok, Gerry. Stop assaulting the bread.

I'd torn the heel from the baguette that sat next to the melon.

- I've just always been interested in church issues, he said.
  The water kept burbling. Who named algae, anyway? Who
  came up with those names?
- I really don't know what they did with him in that pool when
  he was a kid, I said. He probably put his feet in, raced boats,
  looked at tadpoles, pretended to fish, enjoyed being a child.
  I don't know. I don't know, I don't know, and I don't know.
- OK, the Flatmate said quietly. Stick with me.

I let a few minutes go past. I found irregularities in the sound
of the cicadas and put a small amount of cold beer against
my teeth and gums and moved it around and looked up at
the remains of the abbey across the street. The village was
medieval, so every one of its views, every angle, every vista
was already worked over by thousands of eyes. The monks
lifted all this stone, they walked through those stone hall-
ways, past the centuries of prayer accumulated everywhere,
lifting it around their ankles. The sound of the evening continued. How would you get a prayer through all the cicada
noise? Can animals block us out? Would they do that?

He stood there beside me sniffing his hands.

- You would have to be a lay minister, I finally said. The Flatmate looked down at me. He was close enough to smell.

- Why would you have to be a lay minister Gerry? he asked.
- To baptize someone in come.
- Ah ha. Oh yes. I think you're absolutely right with that one, said the Flatmate. He clapped his hands together once. Theologically speaking, I think you're absolutely right. Though the Church of England is very split over this issue.

I stayed out at the table and watched the French street lamp assert its dominance. When he finished making his sandwich the Flatmate yelled out "Rosender!" And when I didn't answer he yelled again: "Rosender! It's me Lysander!" In his John Gielgud voice and then added: "Do you miss the roar of the greasepaint like I do, old plum?"
- Terribly, old mango, I said, as Laurence Olivier. Terribly.

And then he left me alone. A bat turned jagged circles against the last bit of orange sky. The abbey took leave of us in the dark. I pulled the cigarette butt from the melon, in due accordance with the Geneva Convention.

Written by Kevin Fanning

Illustrated by Ian Dingman

It's a routine examination. The getting there and getting back will take longer than the event itself, just a few minutes in between all the other things you'll do that day. Focus on everything after.

You have to explain this to your son so he won't panic on the way there. He's four; he doesn't get details, but he can read faces and knows when to be scared. No shots this time, you say. No pinch? he asks. This is the warning sign he's learned, the lie the nurses telegraph. You'll just feel a little pinch, they say, before the needle goes halfway through his arm. No pinch, you say, no shots. You can see him struggling to believe you, fighting back the fear. What has he already learned about the world? You make promises. We'll get a donut after. I bet the nurses will give you stickers. He still likes stickers.

At the doctor's office he sits on the crumpled paper sheet in his underwear, his impossible stick legs hanging off the ledge. He hardly flinches when the doctor looks in his ears, looks in his eyes. You had a list of questions to ask but didn't write them down and can't remember them now. Something about sleep? Something about school? You tell your son he's doing a really good job. He sits there and stares off into nothing while the doctor listens to his heart. You're doing so good. What kind of stickers do you think the nurses have? The doctor is still listening to your son's heart. He has a look on his face. He is struggling to hear a story whispered in a crowded room. Huh, the doctor says, moving the stethoscope, listening some more.

It could be nothing. He wants to get some tests done. It's just to be sure. There might be something but it could be nothing. You look in the rear view mirror. Your son has chocolate icing all over his face, dinosaur stickers up and down his arms.

You take him back for more tests. The nurse puts stickers with metal nodes on his arms and chest and legs, and then connects wires to the nodes. Your son lies on the table in his underwear, very still. You think of Wolverine, his favourite superhero. It's OK, you say. You're doing a really good job. You look to the nurse for affirmation, but she says nothing. When the tests are over she goes to remove the stickers. She pulls one away from his skin and he screams and starts sobbing. It's OK, you tell her, rushing your hands to hers. We'll take them off at home. But he won't let you. He says it hurts too much. They're on him for a week, flashing on his legs and arms while he's playing with Legos, riding his tricycle, whispering something to the cat. You use Vaseline to slide them away from his skin one night while he sleeps. Their disappearance is the first thing he notices when he wakes. In a dream you sense someone standing by your bed. You open your eyes and it's him, staring at you. What happened to me? he says, holding out his arms.

The specialist calls and says it's lucky. It's great that we caught it this soon. We'll need to do a transplant. He says this is the best-case scenario, all things considered. But how many scenarios are there? You can only think of one. You are outside, trying to hear his voice over the traffic, trying to keep your son from running into the street. The specialist is going to transfer you to his nurse to schedule an appointment to talk about it more. Thank you, you say, but the line is suddenly quiet. You wait, unsure if the conversation is still happening.

What does all this mean, you say, in the specialist's office. You have so many questions, but they all seem too big to ask. Isn't he too young for surgery? No, he says. We do it on children much younger than this. Much. Isn't there a long waiting period? For what, the specialist asks. You don't want to say the word with your son in the room. For a, you say, tapping your finger to your chest. The specialist's eyes pop in understanding. No! He smiles. It's not like that, anymore. We use a cell phone now. A cell phone? He nods. Heart out, cell phone in. He doesn't have to wait, and plus it's like a, a, he stares blankly at you, snapping his fingers. I'm hungry, your son says, what do you have? A green initiative, the specialist says, nodding. I've never heard of this, you say. He takes a pamphlet off the wall and hands it to you. It says *Your Cell Phone Heart*. Should we get a second opinion, you ask. Well, sure, he says. You can do that.

That night, after your son is asleep, the cat at his feet, you enter combinations of words into Google. It's all there. This is a thing that exists. There are support groups, apparently, although you won't be able to see them until you register. You enter your email address and are instructed to check your inbox for the confirmation email, but it's not there.

You schedule the surgery. You try not to think about your son's heart as a clock that is winding down, even though it is, they all are. How do you talk about this with him? What do you say? You tell him he has to go back to the hospital. He stops playing for a minute. The Lego guys are having a fight with the Playmobil guys. No pinch, he says? But there is no language for this. You focus instead on what will happen after. The doctors are going to make you all better. You're going to feel better. You won't get so tired. We'll get you a lot of presents. What do you want? you say. Tell me what you want? He has a long list of things he wants. You would starve yourself, sell your body and blood, use your fingernails to tear a hole in time in order to move that world a little closer to this one. He's still naming things. You don't understand half of what he's saying but it's OK, all of it, it's OK.

He sleeps in your bed the night before the surgery. You would have suggested it, if he hadn't first. It's freezing but he keeps kicking off the covers in his sleep. He generates so much heat, lying next to you. What's normal, you wonder.

In the hospital, when they wheel his bed through the doors to the operating room, you feel the universe slowly spinning away, out into nothing, taking your skin with it.

You sit in the waiting room for hours. The room is wall-papered with dinosaurs driving cars. There's a TV but it's turned off. There are other people sitting there waiting. Everyone is waiting for news. You sit there longer than you can imagine, longer than you have ever waited for anything. Maybe they've forgotten about you. Maybe something's gone wrong. You hear names announced over the loud-speaker. You listen, straining to hear, unable to differentiate one name from another.

A nurse comes to get you and bring you up to his recovery room. Everything went fine, she says, like it's an afterthought, like it's not everything. He's just waking up, she says.

The room is huge and dark and he's all alone in it. You have to climb over wires to get to him. He's so small in his bed, so defeated. The TV is turned on to cartoons and his eyes are pointed in that direction but he's so far away. The wires go into his body and the machines thrum beside him. How bruised and tired his eyes look, the blue veins webbed along his temple and eyelids. He's so fragile and translucent you wonder if he'll really even be there, at the end of your fingertips. You want to hold him but hesitate, not wanting to touch him where it might cause him pain.

Beneath his skin, beneath the scar that's already forming across his chest, you feel the electronic pulse, the sub-space signal that carries all that you are into his body. Your fear, your panic and worry and love, subsumed and translated and sent back out into the world. His signal radiates outward, travelling through every living and non-living thing, off the curve of the earth and out into the universe, out into the unknown, across the impossibly long distance of everything still to come.

He's so far away. You want him to know you're there. You lean in and press your hand to his face. You don't say anything. He looks at you.

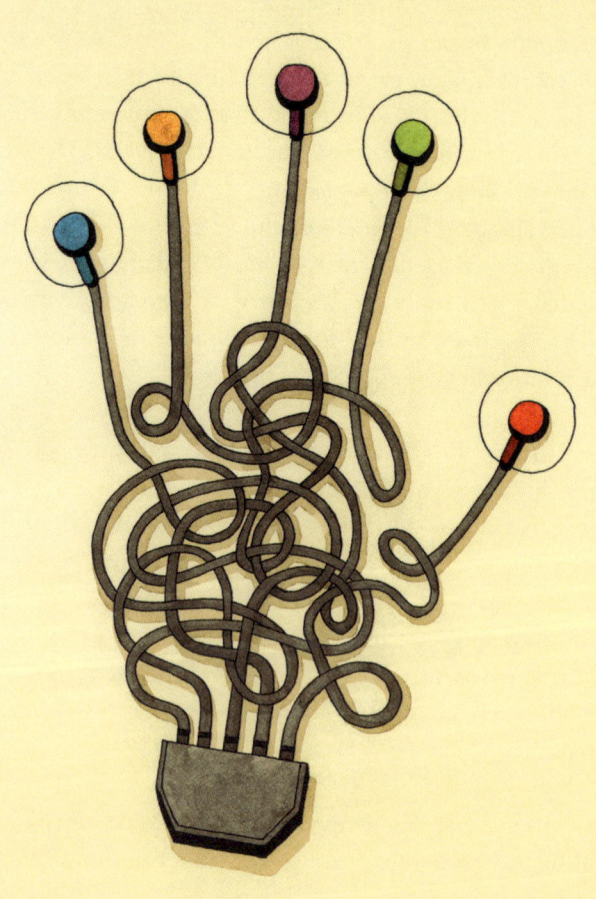

Written by Tess Lynch

Sthe mall Voice

Illustrated by Carson Ellis

On my walk today to Elisabeth's for our sewing circle I was met not only with the usual stares, but outright hostility from one cantankerous gentleman of about twenty years old. His appearance was the typical prideful, immodest garb that the teenagers (and, well, everybody) seem to be drawn to nowadays: torn-up blue jeans, shirt unbuttoned almost to his navel, leather vest outfitted with sinister-looking metal barbs and grommets.

"Happy Halloween!" he shouted at me from his seat outside a grungy café. Of course I do not celebrate Halloween, but I know what it is, I know that it occurs in October and not March; I knew what he thought of me. A cruel joke. I asked him if he knew Jesus, but of course in his ignorance he simply guffawed and told me to get lost. With derision. "Get lost, lady. You're [expletive] nuts."

I straightened my bonnet, my cheeks flaming, trying to decide whether to explain to him that I am following a righteous path, one that is available to all the Lord's children, even the fallen angels who run about with the hair of their chests drawing the attention of strangers, provoking us; I wanted to tell him that I am celebrating my faith and dressing plainly, but as a woman should, in an ankle-length cotton dress I made myself from a Victorian pattern last fall. I wanted to offer up the word of God and the peace that comes with living according to His word. I told him that I would pray for him and he responded with something that I cannot force myself to place on these pages. I walked on, trying to hold myself with dignity and purpose. A tear shed for this man would be too much to afford him.

I thought then of being with my mother and sisters, as I have often recounted to myself in times of hardship and adversity, during my home-schooling in Arkansas. Mother played the dulcimer and gave us music lessons, though only little Anne would ever be able to call from the strings anything that sounded like music. My fingers became calloused and my heart ached to summon the bittersweet sounds that my sister was able to create on that delicate instrument, but I was a hopeless case. My duties fell to taking care of the little ones, four of them being quite a bit younger than I; at this I was more skilled than my two older sisters, perhaps at this alone. Ruth had been blessed with a gift for cooking, and I still have not tasted a better stew than those she would make on Mother's old gas stove. Remembering the warm, sunlit afternoons in Father's study, studying scriptures while a baby laughed from the back lawn: this is all I need to remember God's infinite love and grace.

I arrived at Elisabeth's well kept home in a much better state of mind. Elisabeth had just made some wonderful sweet tea (I must not forget to ask her for the recipe! I thought that I tasted orange blossom) and scones and we ladies set about our work: Mary with her crocheting, Catherine with her knitting needles, and me with a special project.

"Joanna!" exclaimed Catherine. "Is one of your sisters expecting?"

I smiled and held up the wee gingham tunic that was awaiting its gussets. The ladies' eyes turned to me expectantly, but before I could make my announcement little David appeared from the kitchen and glued himself to Elisabeth's side.

"May I have a scone?" he asked, and Elisabeth handed him one and patted him on the bottom so that he would leave.

"We're having a grown-up talk," she explained. "Go back to your studying."

"That's all right!" I said, and extended a hand to David. He has never taken to me, though most children do, but I continued to try to woo him with handmade gifts, sweets, and kindness. David would not leave his mother's side.

"It's okay, David, go see Joanna," Elisabeth urged, but David lowered his eyes and stared at his feet. "He's shy," she explained.

"That's all right," I said, for one without pride can never be wounded. David left the room, slowly, dragging his feet on the way back to his room. When he was safely out of earshot, I leaned towards my friends and whispered, "Jacob and I have been blessed with a child."

"Oh, how wonderful!" crowed Mary, though her words sounded almost hollow, as if she was calling out to a friend on the other end of a vast pasture. She caught herself and lowered her voice, but kept the false thrill. "When are you due?"

I paused. The telling of this part was difficult, complicated. I have suffered for years from what we call "Empty Arms"; I have four young babies in heaven, babies who never took a breath. The Lord called them to Him before they were old enough to be outside my belly, though with each of them but one (poor little Evangeline, who was simply too small) I was able to spend a few lovely moments holding them, tiny pink sea creatures (oh, Lord, please forgive me these thoughts! I banish them but they return: little seahorses, never children, never real babies—forgive me!)—bathing them, baptizing them—before Jacob buried them in their tiny coffins. I sewed tufted velvet cushions and placed my four babies onto them, one by one. I must learn to forgive Mary her disbelief; my bosom friends have suffered with me through many tearful evenings. Though Jacob and I try to eschew modern technology (even the word makes my skin crawl!), we keep an old rotary phone for emergencies, and in moments of weakness I would call my friends, interrupting the precious sleep they're able to secure between waking to attend to their many healthy children, to cry. After I'd hang up the heavy black receiver I would kneel in the kitchen, where Jacob rarely ventures, to pray until my voice was hoarse and my knees bore the marks of the space between wood boards on the floor. After we'd buried sweet little Sarah, I lost faith and endured a spell of feeling as though I had misplaced myself completely. I wouldn't eat; instead of sleeping I would cry or wail. Jacob found me in the attic trying to nurse a rag doll I had made for Sarah, and sent me home to Mother's to recuperate. Here but for the grace of God go I.

"Well, in fact we've been given a boy who was—" I hesitated; it's important to choose the right word, always, as our expressions of our thoughts reflect the sanctuary of our minds. We must keep our thoughts ordered like little chapels. "—He was abandoned. Perhaps orphaned. He was very sick when he arrived. His name is Malachi."

"Oh, I just adore the name Malachi," sighed Catherine. "We almost named Benjamin that, but Richard—" she waved her hand as if to indicate the inferiority of Richard's choice. We never speak ill of our husbands. A wave of the hand is all we permit ourselves.

"Did you adopt him?" pressed Mary. "How old is he? Why didn't you bring him today?" An afterthought: "And congratulations!"

"Well, you remember Jacob's cider experiment," I said, omitting the fact that the cider was alcoholic and Jacob's efforts toward making it had caused us a few rows. "We needed to buy yeast from Kroger's last Tuesday."

"No!" said Elisabeth. "I bought some at the Farmer's Market and have far too much. Next time, ask me!"

"Well, I will," I said, eager to get on with the telling. "But I didn't know, so we had to go to Kroger's. I waited outside, because I just can't stand it in there. And everything's so *expensive*. Anyway, Jacob couldn't find the yeast and I swear he was in there an hour. Perhaps two hours."

"Two hours in Kroger's! I can't even imagine!" Elisabeth wrung her hands. We all try to stay away from the grocery, since we can usually make do with what we grow and make at home.

"I waited outside, Elisabeth, because you know that place is just wretched to me. While I was waiting, I spotted a buggy parked outside with the tiniest little infant in it. He was crying, completely unattended. I watched and waited for almost twenty minutes before I grew too concerned to stand by without offering some help. I approached the buggy and there he was: red-faced, emaciated. My heart just broke for this baby. You can imagine, being mothers yourselves." Silence. "I picked him up and he was starving. And you'll never believe the miracle that happened next."

"I can believe it," said Mary seriously. "God's miracles are often complex. Everything is a mystery."

"Exactly!" I ejaculated, perhaps too loudly. I knew that they would understand: I cherish these women, with their easy sympathy and willingness to include me in their circle even though I previously felt myself to be a childless pariah (of course, now I understand that all of the pain was merely part of God's infinitely wise plan; I would not trade my Malachi for the abatement of that misery, no, I would not trade him for anything. God has given him to *me*). "I held him to me and he stopped crying. He was whimpering, but not crying. He was so hungry. He was just skin and bones. So I took him around the corner, into a private place, and I nursed him. I didn't know I could, but I did, and I nursed him. I knew he was my child."

I stared at them, one at a time, and they at me, all at once. I held myself straight in my chair, the tunic draped over my knees, and dared them to refute me: they would not. They know that I am honest. Mary looked away first. Elisabeth cleared her throat. To see a miracle is to believe it.

"I can show you my milk," I whispered, so little David wouldn't hear. "Look." I produced a pump from my sewing bag and excused myself to the bathroom. My footsteps echoed in the silence. Once I showed them, they would know, just as Jesus summoned fruit from the withered fig tree. In the bathroom, I pumped milk into my jar of pins; no matter, I would boil them later. The milk gave itself readily to the pump; I could have filled the two-gallon bucket I use for washing the floors. I came back into the sitting room, placed the jar on the coffee table, and smiled. Their faces bore shock at God's generosity.

"Wow, Joanna," said Mary. "I suppose it truly is a... a miracle." She pushed the milk back towards me. "For modesty's sake," she said gently. I burned with shame, screwed the lid on the jar and tucked it away; however, articulating the wonder of what had happened was completely necessary, I felt, for them to understand. As I packed up the milk, the rainbow heads of pins bobbing in its murky nourishment, Mary took a deep breath and I steadied myself for what she was about to say.

"Joanna, my only concern here is that, well, perhaps this was someone else's child. How long did you wait before you took him home?"

"Oh, perhaps two hours! After he was fed I brought him back to his buggy and asked the janitor if he knew who the parents were. The janitor didn't know, so I asked the young gentleman at the register. Then I asked a passerby. Oh, Mary, of course I wouldn't kidnap a child! Malachi had been abandoned, and his misfortune became our blessing! Don't you see? This was God's plan—otherwise why would I have been able to nurse him?"

"Did you call the police? Did you put up flyers?" Mary was quite agitated. "What if someone is searching for their child, absolutely frantic? If someone took one of my own… oh, Joanna, you have to return him. You just have to call the police, if you haven't."

I closed my eyes and prayed for Mary to understand. When I opened them, I could see that it was not just Mary who refused to accept my news. The three faces staring back at me were identical in their judgment, strange in their unkindness. I packed up my sewing without a word.

"Please, Joanna, I'm sorry, I didn't mean it," said Mary. "Please stay. Sit down."

I hummed to myself as I turned the knob on the front door, a song Mother used to play on the dulcimer, "Shenandoah." At home, Malachi would be ready for his supper.

Written by Joshua Allen

FINCH'S IS ONLY OPEN FROM 7-9

Illustrated by Scott Campbell

I should've made the appointment with Finch's last night but lost track of time in the darkroom, developing shots from the cameras I stashed in my neighbour's sprinkler system. Also: whiskey, potassium permanganate, T.G.I. Friday's Amaretto Mudslide mixer, warmed under a dim red light, serve neat.

So I had to call early this morning (Finch's is only open from 7–9) to arrange for an escort. I was hoping to get NO. 104 since her bustiness is high and chattiness low, but ended up with NO. 9921. I'd been stuck with him once before and was dismayed to learn he was a *joke teller*. But when you're blindfolded and cuffed in the back of a minivan, you're pretty much at the whim of the driver.

He picks me up, puts on the restraints, applies the blindfold (padded and chilled), and then drives around for like fifteen minutes, constantly turning, backing up, stopping suddenly, a handful of u-turns, *What'd one Polack say to the other Polack,* then we ease down into what I happen to know is a gated parking garage. NO. 9921 takes me to the elevator and turns a key to unlock the fifth floor button. He walks me down a hallway to a door and knocks an uncoded knock, or what is designed to appear uncoded. And here's Finch, wrapping up a phone call and punching something into an adding machine.

(Finch: Always younger than expected, his face queerly flat and empty, what is that a moustache or what, breakable fingers, teeth out of a magazine, always with the three-piece suits.)

He's got his little apartment set up like an office with fluorescent lights and cubicles and a water cooler and a ditto machine and framed motivational posters. There is the clack of typing and the burble of electronic phone rings. NO. 9921 told me how Finch had just fired his millionth receptionist and sure enough there's a naked mannequin torso stashed behind the little greeting desk. He's got the right hand rigged to a pulley system and he makes the thing wave at me when I come in. "Hi, big boy!" he says in his sexy lady voice.

"Ma'am," I say, tipping the hat I'm not wearing.

"So, Mister Allen," Finch says. "Feeling lucky."

"Definitely feeling a feeling," I say.

"I'd love to talk about these feelings."

"I think I told you about my dead grandpappy and how his leg got chewed up in a farming thing and how he could feel atmospheric changes where his leg used to be?"

"And maybe you somehow inherited this phantom leg?"

"Just saying there's forces we don't know anything about."

Finch gives my shoulder a good squeeze. "That's why we're here, my friend. Now tell me all about it."

"Five thousand dollars on July the 11th. Partly cloudy with an isolated shower or thunderstorm in the afternoon. Winds west-northwest at five to fifteen miles per."

Finch gives me a little look before jotting it down. "That thunderstorm is a pretty bold call."

"You gonna keep jawing or you gonna place the bet?"

"Who says I can't do both," Finch says with a wink, handing his note off to an assistant.

And now I'm all nervous. Now I want to call Eller and tell him to call the whole thing off. Just unplug the device and haul it back out to the tool shed. We should wait a few months, let Finch get distracted, check the almanac for a more plausible day. I mean seriously what was I thinking.

Written by Joe Meno

A
HELIum RIDE

Illustrated by Oliver Jeffers

Helium can be expensive: so the critics say, but thousands of bicycle enthusiasts use helium to fly their bicycles in the sky anyway. For safety, most bicycle enthusiasts wear the standard metal bolt helmet, quite similar to a deep sea diver's, when pedaling high above the city's parks, statues, and buildings. There is almost always a long line at the stores that sells helium: true bicycle enthusiasts bring a long poem to read while waiting. The helium itself comes in small orange and blue boxes. The helium must be unfolded like a flag before you can use it. It is soft and flat and hardly feels like a noble gas. You attach the helium, like a cape, securing it around your neck. Then you must climb aboard the right kind of bicycle, one that is very light and supported by several small silver balloons. You are already wearing your bolt helmet, which is quite heavy and acts as an important counter-balance. Without the heavy, golden bolt helmet you will assuredly drift up into the cloudlessness of outer space.

A helium ride may be the perfect first outing for a young couple, especially during the brisk months of autumn. Young men and women, silent on first dates, will often go for a bicycle ride somewhere high above the glassy skyscrapers and nervous-looking masses that crowd the city's thoroughfares. The young couples will not ride above the county medical waste disposal plant, which from high up, looks like a lovely garden but immediately burns the eyes with its stolid fumes. They will also avoid pedaling out over the ocean and the blackened confines of the helium factory, which looks quite sinister, its great smokestacks flaring with bluish-grey gas. The young couple may instead prefer to land at one of the city's many balloon cafes, which are floating restaurants, and which provide many delectable desserts and coffees.

The young couple may then share their first kiss staring down at the distant city, moved by the immeasurable silence, positioning their feet very near each other's without touching. They may enjoy the scarcity of rats at this great height, the rats which in the city are so abundant and aggressive, having been known to bite unsuspecting citizens' necks, legs, and faces. The young couple may press their bare feet together and prepare their faces to be kissed. Kissing at that altitude may be difficult but not altogether impossible. The bolt helmet, which bicycle enthusiasts wear and is almost always painted gold for a high degree of visibility, features a circular glass window which may be opened, pressure and height permitting. Kissing is best performed between zero and sixty feet. Above that, there may be complications due to the highly compressed atmosphere which may destroy the helium enthusiast's ears, eyes, and lungs. At the proper height however, the glass portal may be easily opened, and the young couple may or may not decide to take the opportunity to whisper something romantic or make a small sensitive joke before they extend their necks and touch their mouths together with their lips. For most bicycle enthusiasts enjoying a helium ride, drifting above the city with your date nearby, will provoke strong feelings of romance and an intense attraction. The apparent lack of air may impair judgment however.

Some things to avoid when enjoying a helium ride:

1. Fireworks—Though fireworks may seem exciting, with their flashes of silver and purple clouds crackling in the air, unfortunately, fireworks have been known to burn the helium enthusiast's extremities.

2. Birds—Most birds are quite docile and friendly, though some birds, specifically gulls and crows have been known to attack in formations single bicyclists who appear weak or tired, and often time, bicyclists who are very short or elderly.

3. Dangerous bicycle feats like figure-eights and loop-de-loops—Riding a bicycle in the sky is very different than riding a bicycle on the ground. For example, a dangerous bicycle feat on the ground which fails does not share the same deadly consequences as a failed bicycle feat in the air. For the helium enthusiast's safety, it is important to always remember you are floating.

4. Smoking and/or heavy meals—The smallest spark may surely ignite the veil of helium you will be wearing around your neck. Be careful to avoid the tiniest flame or you will surely explode in a bluish cone of fire. Also avoid heavy meals, specifically starches and fattening sweets. A sudden increase in the helium enthusiast's weight may or may not create a dangerous imbalance, which will certainly end in a fatal crash.

5. Airplanes—Airplanes always have the right of way. Due to their great size, airplanes and other kinds of air traffic can be hard to maneuver. They may or may not exert a gravitational pull due to their jet stream. Always avoid all forms of air traffic—airplanes, balloons, and gliders.

6. Horseplay—Do not poke, prod, or jab at your fellow enthusiast's bolt helmets.

7. Ghosts—The physical manifestations of the recently deceased may appear as great silver cubes at various locations throughout the lower atmospheres. Though many of these silver cubes may appear friendly, glowing and flashing talkatively, other ghosts may be extremely lonely and unpleasant to interact with. Other still, more desperate,

may attach themselves to the unsuspecting enthusiast's feet.

Some things to exclaim while enjoying a helium ride:
1. "Look at that!"
2. "Look! Look how small everything is!"
3. "I love you!"
4. "I am really flying!"
5. "Look out below!"

Some things to talk about while enjoying a helium ride:

1. The Sky—The sky makes a very enjoyable subject to discuss: its colour, the size and shape of its clouds, what those clouds remind you of, whether a storm may be in sight.

2. Kissing—It is entirely appropriate to mention the kinds of kissing you like. You may discuss your favourite memory of kissing, where you shared your most enjoyable kiss, you may even talk about your least pleasant experience and thereby create a connection with your date based on personal feelings and memories.

3. Helium—When using helium, you may discuss its properties: apart from lifting dirigibles and bicycles, helium has many other uses. For example, liquid hydrogen is a very popular rocket fuel. Helium is used as the pressurant or the gas which fills the rocket tank as the fuel is being used. Just think: if you didn't have enough helium, what could you use instead—something else that's a gas at the temperature of liquid hydrogen? I don't believe there is such a gas.

4. Human relationships—Perhaps an interesting story demonstrating the complexities of human relationships would make an interesting point of discussion. For example: an anecdote that describes how you easily relate to lower

classes of people; maids, butlers, servants, cooks, waitresses, mail carriers, teachers, professional comedians, professional musicians, sewer workers, city officials, clerks.

5. God—Helium rides often induce enthusiasts to ponder thoughts of God, Life, and their own Existence. Perhaps a cloud reminds you of God's fluffy white beard. Use this opportunity to find out how your date feels about serious issues and whether or not you are religiously compatible, which scientists claim is just as important as it used to be.

Perhaps helium rides are best known for the splendid and colourful air mirages that often appear due to cloud refraction, helium fumes, and the loss of blood to the head. While riding above the open landscape of the city, the young couple may spot glowing winged female children, sun-light-speckled clipper ships, or thousands of dappled gravestones. Many helium enthusiasts have claimed, when riding alone in the cloudy sky, to have heard voices and to have witnessed uncanny events, which days and nights later, have mysteriously come to pass: meeting a stranger, being hit by an automobile, falling from an open window. Some helium devotees even believe these unfathomable illusions appearing at such a great height are actually other people's undreamt dreams. Whether or not this is true, for nearly a century, fans of aviation have enjoyed these strange, unpredictable images which helium enthusiasts and aviators have both carefully documented.

Popular involvement in helium recreation dates to the Helium Act of 1925 which authorized the Bureau of Mines to build and operate a large-scale helium extraction and purification plant, which then offered helium to the public at an affordable price. From 1929 until 1960 the federal government was the only domestic helium producer, though participation in helium recreation at the time was quite small. With the creation of the helium bolt helmet and the congressional amendment to the Helium Act, which provided incentives to natural gas producers for the production of helium, this miracle gas could be now purchased by the general public at discount rates. Ballooning and helium bicycle rides soon became the popular sports young couples know and love today.

Though helium rides can be amazing, enjoyable, and generally safe, a dangerous pattern has begun to occur among certain young and often troubled couples: a familiar story regarding one particular young couple on their last helium ride gives the helium hobbyist pause to think. The young couple ascended to sixty feet and whispered their charming enchantments to one another, holding hands and pointing at flocks of sparrows passing-by. *Look,* they said. *Those sparrows look like children playing musical instruments. It is so beautiful up here. Let's never return to earth.* The young couple opened the glass portals of their helmets and shared an intimate, touching kiss. From there, the couple ascended another fifty feet, well into the upper atmosphere. At one hundred and ten feet, the couple shared their most personal and final secrets, once again, opening their glass portals. At this point, decompression set in and like two golden balloons, the young couple's helmets filled with air. As expected, their helmets and heads swelled greatly in size, and the young couple, only giggled at their strange appearances. Their lungs and hearts, also expanded greatly, and now both the young man and young woman were filled with an amazing euphoria. Letting go of their weighted bicycles, the young couple grasped hands and together drifted higher and higher into the dark, indifferent boundaries of the atmosphere. Though suddenly happy and quite in love, the couple must have surely died before drifting into outer space. Many critics of helium rides contend that this kind of "accidental suicide" happens too often and even enthusiasts of the sport agree. Helium rides often attract too many, young, impulsive, and suicidal couples, who have abused helium recreation as their means of their deaths for far too long. Self-asphyxiation at the upper registers of the atmosphere should not be seen as romantic. You must know those last feelings of calm are only helium-induced illusions: You are not a bird. You are not an angel.

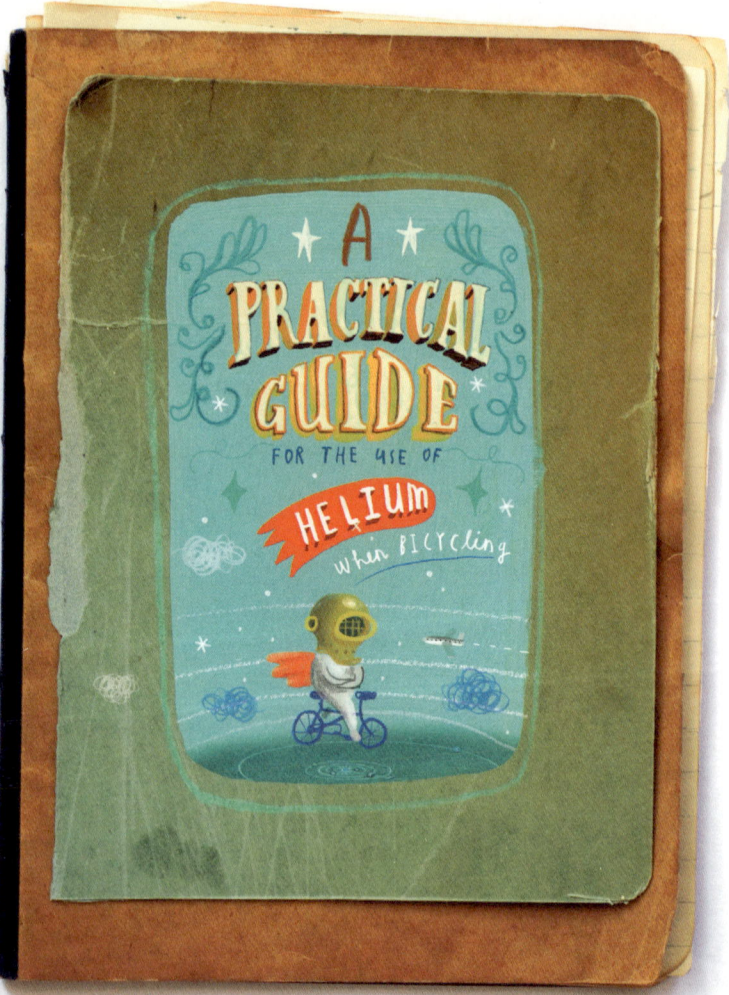

A

PRACTICAL
GUIDE
FOR THE USE OF
HELIUM
when BICycling

Written by Evie Wyld

FORGOTTEN PLACE,
SYDNEY

Illustrated by Hannah Waldron

My great aunt Merle is not dead. She has just been repositioned in an old persons' home not far away from Glebe, but the air in her house is long dead. She lived in there, in what used to be suburbia, from the time she was first married. She brought up her children there, sat out the war and won it.

The hallway has the feel of being in dense undergrowth, weak light comes in through the green glass above the front door, and the carpet soaks it up, a thick dark brown shag which feels, on bare feet, damp and warm like a living thing. White plastic shutters, the kind you might get in a hospital, have been attached in the doorways of the bedrooms—but this is only since Merle's grandchild came to stay and wanted privacy—before then the whole house was door-less, I'm told, just a shower curtain that you pulled around a hip bath.

There's a wet room, with a mildewed sink, a yellow hose hanging above a plastic garden chair for a shower. Merle was living on her own, and there is no shutter on the wet room, which is directly opposite the front entrance, via the long dark hallway. I like the idea that you would open the front door to Merle sat on the garden chair, in the olive green of her bathroom suite, a large old woman like a trompe l'oeil. On the window sill of the wet room, the saved leaves of white and green soaps and several different coloured toothbrushes, bristles splayed. The actual toilet is in the backyard, which is concreted with the odd burst of razor grass that has pushed through the cracks made by the morton bay fig in next door's garden.

The narrow rooms have low unplastered ceilings, made for people who don't look up. Old bills piled neatly on a bookcase, and on top of them, a dried cat's shit. Patience; Merle's cat has been re-homed, apparently, though my uncle said it with a small glance away, which leads me to believe old Patience may have met with the sharp end of a shovel, perhaps in her very backyard where she could be tidily dispatched of. I don't feel too bad for her, she liked to bite the back of your neck if you sat on the sofa, or if you dared think she was a cat for stroking, she'd go for the thin skin on the inside of your arm. She would have appreciated the violence of her death, I am sure of it.

In the kitchen, the miniature hot plate, the slow cooker, the microwave. The food left in the freezer testifies to the meals made in that kitchen. Pre-cooked lasagne, fisherman's pie, liver and bacon with suet dumplings. Everything is for re-heating, nothing is raw. None of the food I think of as being Australian. No passion fruit, no mango, no pink-shelled prawns. The fridge/freezer is a recent gift from Merle's children, and it looks out of place, a sky scraper amongst tents. It must have towered above Merle, and reminded her that times had changed. This is no kerosene, squat cold-box. It puffs its white chest out into the kitchen, stands head and shoulders above the olive green vacuum cleaner, the brown microwave.

The pictures and statues of Jesus and Our Lady of the Sacred Heart, old pieces from the forties, a daguerreotype of someone dressed up as the blessed virgin, many times kissed, clouded, even inside its leather box. There are eyes everywhere, rolling upwards.

A few family photographs are hung just above eye level. They are of the grandchild and some are of great uncle Jack, dressed in his uniform, hat brim curved to the side of his head in the Australian way, nose as prominent as a beak. A photograph of a baby, sitting in a bucket with a sailor's hat on, smiling with its coloured-in lips and eyes.

The smell is of closeness and heat, and of the wrong uphol-stery for a hot country. Moist dust sticks to glass surfaces. Cockroaches lie upturned, camouflaged by the brown swirl of the carpet. Formica is the dominant textile used for soft furnishings. It provides a protective layer over chairs and mattresses, so that when you sit or lie the noise is of air es-caping, and when you stand up you leave behind the print of your buttocks.

For the seventeen years since great uncle Jack died, Merle has lived alone in this darkness. Probably, she loved the house because it was her home, and in its crumbling grout work was the breath of her children and the man she loved. What is left is a crust; somewhere that has seen deaths and births and fires and snow, that has absorbed family arguments and singing, and the smell of a thousand baked dinners. Violence and love-making, proposals and Monopoly, the intense heat of summer and the mild fug of winter. And no one will want to live there now. The house may be gutted and someone may start over again in its empty shell, whitewash the walls, build an indoor toilet, knock through to make it open plan, let the light in, let the air in. But more likely the whole lot will be flattened, easily, and something more habitable will grow in its place. Thankfully.

But what if you could save the house, what if it was to remain a museum to the people who have lived there. I want to be able to appreciate that once the important thing was to have a door to keep the strangers out, to keep the family in, but when I look at the acid yellow paintwork, the collections of grubbed kewpie-dolls and the biscuity corners of the living room, I'm relived that someone might start again from clean scratch, that the house will be absorbed quietly into the city and no one, except Patience, if she really is alive, will miss it.

Written by Ronnie Scott

Illustrated by William Exley

The dissemination of my brother's will had largely been a bust. Other than bequeathing his record collection to "all dudes globally" and a light-up sign above his bed that said *No Fat Chicks!* to our mother, the only unambiguous thing—and this was only owing to my historically strong patience—was that the job of throwing out everything in his apartment fell to me. Late on the day I did that, my wife and the round child inside her eased up from the floor and she felt around in the back pocket of my jeans for our car keys. As I was bent over a final "file box", which was turning out to be an unorganised set of cardboard beer coasters he had leavened over the years from bars, my back pocket was tight, and it took her a while. I liked it. "And I'd stay longer, too, but the thing seems to need some cookie dough," my wife said. "Don't call your mouth 'the thing'," I said. "To me, it's so much more than that." Now we knew it was a boy in her, my wife's job today had been to sit there and call out stupid names for babies while I tied off garbage bags. "Perineum" was the one we liked. "*Very* continuous," I said was the appeal. And now that she had gone I wished that I had brought my iPod.

I was only going through those final files because in a similar box earlier there had been a couple of thoughtlessly-preserved importantish papers, and it was only a lot later that I began to qualify that word differently, as he had died. And now, near the bottom of the box, there was an even worner-looking folded paper—which turned out just to be a tourist map of our city.

The thing that made me look at it a little longer than I would have was that my brother had lived here in our city all his life; which was not that he had settled, but more because

I couldn't even imagine him organising an itinerary into his hand. There was my street, I saw, and the ten blocks between us, and I thought of how often he had ordered my wife and I unasked-for pizzas right on closing time. I was lucky I had found a wife who had a stupid sense of humour. Most recently we'd come home one night to ten plastic lawn chairs stacked against our door, which I had made my wife step away from and allow me to unstack. But it had been she, with the child inside her, who had gone carrying our broom all the way to my brother's place, and propped it against his door; and then she who had, when a half-awake bleached-blond girl opened the door instead of my brother, filled a tea towel up with ice cubes and held it on the girl's broomed head. I visually traced the road between our house and this apartment, and pictured my wife giggling down that line.

That was how I noticed he had dashed a rhomboid of fluro ink into the road, the same size as the nib on a high-lighter pen. With a muscle memory from my word-search habit—actual crosswords I find very hard—I searched the map concentrically, and I saw that the other ink marks, of which there were a number, became scarcer the farther into the suburbs I searched.

I felt a little sick when I was looking at the dashes. Not because they were weird, exactly, but because *I* was being weird. Most of my brother's things had seemed to be things, unimbued, but everyone has their special somethings that they do choose to keep private, and I had feared that eventually I would see one. I had felt ashamed of my own special somethings before I wound up, finally, in a good relationship, which is when I learned, pretty late in the game for pretty much a happy person, that winding up with somebody isn't about eliminating your special somethings, and leaving a kind of spotless Siamese union in their place. It's about allowing for the spaces between you to live and lie. Sometimes I like to poo in the shower, which is why I always lock the bathroom door. My wife must have a different something, because she leaves the door unlocked, and even when I don't sneak in and watch her showering, she's told me that she peeps around the shower glass to check. That is why I only do it once every few weeks or so, these things tending naturally to routine themselves.

I poured myself a glass of water, and then threw that last glass into a garbage bag. I emptied the coasters into the garbage bag. I collapsed the file box into the garbage bag, and I tied this last bag off. My wife had already driven home the items I was keeping, and I folded the map into my jacket pocket now. I took the bag out to the garbage chute and dropped it inwards, struggling to touch as little in the chute-room as I could. And then I closed the thin door to the apartment behind me, depressing the lock for the last time; and then I slid his keys under the door for his landlord, for whom I had expressed luck in finding another tenant, because on the phone he'd sounded unprepared for my brother's death.

Walking home, I thought of other good names for my baby: "Greasenut", "Sackface", "Gunt". These names were good because my wife would like them. The first night I had met her, I was drunk at a nice function, and she had belted herself thickly at a high point on her stomach, so it looked as if the two triangular bottoms of her button-up shirt were actually features of her skirt. She said hello to me at the bar. "No, *you* are!" I said to her. "I'm sorry," I said. "I think you're amazing, and it's amazing that you've given your vulva its own little collar."

And the rest is a long story devoted equally to things like house buying and also semi-seriously trying to pee on each other while we were walking home from somewhere drunk. In fact, she had initially had trouble disguising her pregnancy because people noticed how she wasn't drinking, her major quality, and we would shiningly say that she was detoxing "for her health". "My face," I thought. "We could call him 'My face'. So that if he's slow getting up for school, we can yell 'Come on my face!' up the stairs." Not that our house had stairs. Sometimes I can't even wait to tell things I've thought of to my wife, and I have to text her just before I walk in the door. Meanwhile, my poor brother is lying in a coffin and doesn't have a baby to be born.

I passed a little dead-end street I always passed, and thought of passingly; a funny accident of subdivision which had one unremarkable house on it, and a lot of unbuildable lots. And from memory, memorially, from when I'd searched before, I somehow knew that this street was marked on my brother's map.

Reading the map more carefully as I left the cross street's lighting, I noticed that the rhomboid mark of highlighter pen lined up with the one unremarkable house, of course.

There was a big soily pot out the front of the house, with the grey rope of a dead basil plant winding out.

I wanted to knock on the door and I was near it, so I did.

A woman opened the door who had the limp type of short hair that women use a hair straightener to make. I have always wanted to straighten my own hair, but my own hair is far too short. The only thing I've ever used a hair straight-ener to do was scare my wife in the shower by holding a plugged-in electrical object at her.

"I know who *you* look like," the woman said. I look sort of like Seth Green, but of course she meant my brother.

"There's no easy way to say this," I began. No female had shown up at the funeral of my brother, and who knew what the hundreds of numbered names in his cell phone really meant. But the woman's unimpressed expression said she knew. "It was probably a lot harder for you to hear," she said. She allowed me to come in.

The features of her lounge room were two cold, open picture windows, which let you look at the backs of people's fences; at their yards. I sat down at the table that was under both these windows, and she set a kettle boiling before sitting down with me. She lit up a cigarette from the packet on the table. Instinctively and dumbly, I made a big round shape out of my hands, but my wife and the thing we made were safe from the smoke in our home. "Now, here, how are you doing?" the woman said when she had sucked it.

Because for a silent time I thought approximately of nothing: "I'm excited for the future," I blurted out. And then I came up quickly with a considered-seeming phrase: "I'm not sure what the world will be without my brother in it." This was a good, ambiguous answer for a person whose position was mysterious to me. I hadn't known, I had admitted, what my brother would be to my baby. I had hoped he would become "Uncle Cool Vibes", cool vibes, great uncle, basically the last among us to be young. But I feared he would remain young in the ways that distance an uncle. And of course, this very outcome was now the other, *other* unambiguity.

"Well," she said, and thought, dragged, blew. "Speaking as a person whose world has almost *never* had your brother in it, it's really just a nice slice of fine life either way. I'm glad he had a brother. I have a really shitty brother."

She started telling me a bunch of shit about her shitty brother. When I tried to pick it up, I had not been listening for far too long. "And that is why my family still *has* a Christmas, but doesn't *call* it Christmas," she finished.

"That's amazing," I said. She looked up sharply. "Terrible," I said, and put my hands down on the table with an exaggerated smack. My thick wedding ring clicked on it, and the woman noticed. "I should pour us some tea," she said. "No, that's fine. Just have some yourself later," I said. "I will definitely do that," the woman said.

"Good," I said. "Now look, I don't know if you're wondering how I know who you are, but—" The woman looked briefly hurt. "I wonder if you know what this map is of my brother's." I removed it from my pocket and unfolded it for her. She bounced her flat eyes briefly off it. "Sex map," the woman said.

"What?"

"Yeah," she told me.

I think I was a little discombobulated. "A sex map. What is they?" I said. And she explained to me how sex maps were things that sometimes people had, and, closely reading it, that she hoped the house where her fucking friend Lucy lived had previously been tenanted by a woman that was unambiguously a stranger to herself, because—. I hoped that her friend Lucy had been excellent to my brother. I wondered whether Lucy, or this woman, or the other, or the other, or the other woman, or the other, or another, was the dragon of my brother's map; and who was the hippo, and who was the cannibal, and who had been the greenery, and who had been the asp. When I got home, I slammed the door. "Hello?" I called. "Hello," she said. "Hello?" she said. "Hello?" I said. "Hello? Hello? Hello?!!!" This is a game we played where we pretended we were both invisible. I dropped my jacket, rolled my underpants and jeans off, and scrunched under the bedcovers in just my socks and shirt. "Fuckhead," my wife said, "that's one thing you're going to have to stop doing if we have a baby in the house." "If?" I said. "*If?*" "Nigh-nigh," my wife said sleepily, falling back to sleep. "Nigh-nigh," I said. I waited sixty seconds, and then necked up to her ear. "You'll never wake up," I whispered. But now my wife was definitely sleeping. I took the hand of the arm that I had laid across the round thing and ran it down around her thighs. And I was glad I had drawn my own sex map while my pen was still black and bold, and that I followed it so blindly past her cervix. In these places elephants are born, in these places scorpions are born, here dog-headed beings are born.

Written by Nicolas Burrows

HEAVY, SEVERED, AT THE SHOULDERS

Illustrated by Maxwell Holyoke-Hirsch

After they had been to see the Hollow Head and the tall White Tower and the Smooth Rock lying down on the beach, there was not really much else to do. She read to him out loud, but he was conscious of a dull, rhythmic sound that seemed lost and far away, and it kept running into his thoughts more and more. He felt bitter and strode off along the beach, keeping in the shadow of the forest and reaching out a hand now and then to feel the briny-damp bark of the shoreline trees. He raked his eyes across the sky, and through the mist he could make out sea lions clustered on a large rock, slithering and baying at the sun.

The rusted ship stood silent on the cliff like a drab metaphor. He looked back towards the beach but she had already gone up to the house. Air moved like a heavy thing out from the forest.

All at once the sand felt unbearably hot and coarse beneath his feet, and he moved further into the shade of the trees. He took off his shoes and laid them solemnly on the soft, dark earth. He could still make out the house, and looking back there he shivered and felt uneasy. A radio was playing in the kitchen and he caught bits of talking and tinned music filtering through the low branches. Instinctively he walked in the opposite direction. He saw a tall flowering grass that he did not know the name of, and rolled it between his finger and thumb. Something gnawed at his conscience. He did not know the names of any of the things that grew around him.

The fur on his arms was beginning to grow thicker and lighter, and as the sunlight streamed through the holes in the clouds it already glowed gold at the tips. Thoughts fluttered like tiny hummingbirds whirring in and out of sight and he suddenly wanted to say something dramatic and real, but he did not want to say it to her.

The magic of the forest gathered about him and became the collected static of a hundred thunderstorms. Songs collected like pools in his throat and welled up and out of his mouth.

They spilled quiet and heavy to the floor and were lost among the broad-leaved plants and browned moss. Perhaps they would reach the tiny ears of young spiders, but there was no way to tell.

Written by Richard Milward

Illustrated by Adrian Johnson

There's no cure for heartbreak, except possibly suicide or superhuman sex with a stranger. Martin, being a shy fellow
at heart, daren't drag his Swiss army knife across his jugular, and he daren't drag himself out to one of the nightspots
either, for fear of coming home alone and then having no
choice but to drag the Swiss army knife across his jugular,
on a drunken whim. At the minute, he doesn't trust himself
in the presence of evil spirits and mixers. Or pissed-up, up-
for-it, ugly women.

Martin's ex—a bonny blonde from Billingham—caught
him off-guard four years back, smacking her lips on him at a
half-empty discotheque in town. Even more surprising was
her wanting to settle down with him, in spite of his night
dribbling, and his nervous twitches.

But now she's gone. Absence certainly makes the heart
grow fonder, but breaking up with someone makes the heart
grow big, black batwings, flapping violently inside your chest.
Panic is first to kick in—suddenly your future's in shreds;
suddenly you've got to start showering and changing your
socks more. Next to come is the moping and moaning—an-
noyingly, the two traits least likely to endear you to a new
suitor. Finally, you get regret and remorse, as you resort yourself to the fact they're not coming back.

Martin likes to think his ex is suffering just as badly as
him but, merely a week after the big breakup, Lorna was
seeing another man. Martin wonders if he should be suspi-
cious about this. He's a very superstitious person. Then again,
single bonny blondes have no bother getting strangers into
bed for superhuman sex. Shy, ageing twenty somethings like
Martin, on the other hand, are the ones more inclined towards the suicide. They start weighing up the pros and cons

of dragging Swiss army knives across their jugulars, dying alone in one fell swoop rather than gradually dying alone over the course of a long, lonely lifetime.

Martin doesn't want to die, though. Martin's a closet optimist. Or, at least, Martin's a fantasist. The night he and Lorna split, Martin trudged up to his bedroom, to wank over a flurry of phantasmagorical females on his computer. He convinced himself he'd be in bed with a silicon-implanted Sindy before heartbreak could even get a look-in. But, six weeks down the line, he's hardly had a nod or a wink off a lady. One night he tried to talk to one in a shop, but he ended up coming across as backward.

Oh, Martin. The worst part is when the fantasies turn dark. When you're suffering from depression, for some reason your brain turns into a professional wind-up merchant. Martin's head feels heavy with Technicolor images of Lorna being touched-up by her new man; or Lorna laughing too loudly at one of his shit quips; or Lorna putting effort into oral sex for once. Martin's gutted that she might've bought a new bra and knickers since splitting up with him, and that her new man's seen them and he hasn't. Even the thought of the new man knowing Lorna's full name makes Martin want to stick screwdrivers in his eyes. She's got one of the best full names he's ever heard.

Welling up, Martin reaches over to his pine-effect chest of drawers. He waits for his left cheek to stop twitching, then he removes two leather dolls from the uppermost drawer, and places them on his duvet.

Martin knew three years at fashion college would pay off. He made the dolls last night in a feverish, lovelorn frenzy, stitching together off-cuts of beige leather and buttoning some eyeballs. The first doll—a female—has the looks and vital statistics of a Hollywood starlet: lovingly brushed blonde hair, pink cross-stitched lips, plaggy emerald eyes, and an 8cm waist under big titties. She wears tiny appliquéd knickers, with a dainty L sewn in. The other doll—a male—has been roughly botched together, with only a few strands of woolly hair, lumpy wadding, and red, glassy eyeballs. This doll wears a pair of tiny brown Y-fronts, which say the word TWAT. While Martin has never met Lorna's new man, he knows he's got the proportions right: big head, small knob.

As Martin's eyes fill with tears again, suddenly there's sixteen voodoo dolls spinning on his bedcovers. He rubs them back to two, and sniffs up a sluggish bogey. The wind-up merchant in Martin's skull fires another image of Lorna and her new man—high as kites on honeymoonshine—settling down for their seventh shag of the evening. Quivering with rage, Martin slides down the dolls' underwear, and grudgingly slides the TWAT one on top of the L one.

"Uh uh uh," Martin mumbles between sobs, making the two dolls shag. He spins them into different positions—positions he tried himself with Lorna, but could never pull off.

Thirty seconds into the simulated sex, Martin makes the TWAT figure shudder and speak in a comedy twat voice: "Uh uh oh, shit, not again, I'm sorry Lorna, I've only gone and cummed too early again!"

Martin makes L roll off the TWAT, exasperated. This gives Martin momentary satisfaction, until the thought of another (real) man's cream inside his ex-girlfriend spoils the mood completely.

Slapping himself, Martin stands and paces about his

room, trying to forget. But the more he tries to forget, the
more he ends up remembering: certain shoes; her areolae;
the smell of behind her ears; holding one of her eyelashes in
his hand; the time they went to the supermarket and the bag
handles snapped.

All those good times are gone now.

Martin should really be out looking for work—or, better still, a new lover—but heartbreak renders even the most
conscientious folk useless. He glances at himself in the
stretch mirror Lorna forced him to buy for £44.99. He tries
to adopt a macho pose, puffing his chest out, but he gets distracted by Lorna's greasy fingerprints still touching the glass.
He can't believe the fucking mirror's getting more attention
off her than him!

Close to breaking point, Martin throws himself back
onto his bed. He throttles the TWAT figure between forefin-
ger and thumb. He presses so hard, the tiny neck stitches
click, snapping open.

After body slamming the doll back onto the soft duvet,
Martin smokes a fag. His nervous twitches cause all sorts of
SOS smoke signals while he puffs it. Having something to do
with his hands, lips and lungs keeps his mind off Lorna for
three minutes, but then he can't help stubbing the Lambert
into the TWAT's chest, and it all comes back to him.

Still twitching, Martin takes the voodoo doll over to his
windowsill. He drags the sash open, and stares out across
the drab street corner, where people are zipping about, no
doubt without the burden of any heartbreak. No doubt on
their way to ravish new lovers. Look at their jaunty footsteps; the bastards.

Taking the purple Clipper back out of his jeans, Martin

sucks more filthy, gluey tears down his throat. He dangles the TWAT figure from its foot, upside down, and sparks up the lighter. As the flames tickle the TWAT's head, black magic smoke billows out of the open window. The fire alarm stuck to Martin's ceiling turns a blind eye.

Before long, the doll's head and torso have turned to cinders. Martin dunks the TWAT into a glass of day-old Ribena (as if he's a torturer, drowning the TWAT for answers, eg: 'What have you got that I haven't got?'/'Why don't you just fuck off?'), extinguishing the last of the embers. Then, Martin lays the toy down on the windowsill, like a burns victim on a cold, mucky mortuary slab.

Martin considers texting Lorna but, at best, he'll receive a one-word answer, with nowhere near enough xxxs on the end of it. It's a cruel sort of algebra, the sudden depletion of xs on the ends of your ex's texts once you've broken up. Martin fucking hates algebra. He's a fashion man, is Martin.

As one final act of revenge/catharsis/daftness, Martin leaves a little cross-stitched x between the TWAT's legs, when he snips the doll's dick off. He chucks the shrunken fabric cock out of the window, to next door's dogs. Then, he slams the sash shut, feeling all masculine, having well and truly got one over on a little dolly.

No sooner has the window thudded shut, when Martin's bedroom door swings suddenly open. Standing on the threshold is a severely distressed young female. She blinks at Martin with tears streaming down her face. Her mascara's running everywhere, causing a sloppy, black action painting on her cheeks, framed by lovingly brushed blonde hair.

Martin's stomach drops.

Despite the action painting, Lorna's easily recognisable

by her pink lips and emerald eyes, although her titties aren't quite as big as the voodoo doll has it.

Rendered immobile by the sight of his ex in distress, Martin feels his machismo crawl away, underneath his bed. He adopts a silly puppy dog expression, smiling far too much, trying to disguise his rage and depression as passion and approachability. He wipes away his tears.

"Help, help," Lorna squeals, swaying about. She doesn't even notice his tears—or the smiling, for that matter. She's too busy with her own tears.

"I'll do anything," Martin says, a bit desperate.

"It's Darryl," Lorna sniffs, meaning her new man.

"Mnh."

Darryl punches Martin in the chest, telepathically.

Without another word, Lorna staggers off down the corridor. Martin follows her, like a lapdog, or a jester poised to tend to the queen's every need. While put-on rage is an unattractive quality in men, put-on helplessness is even worse. Nevertheless, it's hard not to appear needy when you're needy.

Martin tails her down the corridor, transfixed by that mole on her neck he'd forgotten about.

"Get an ambulance," she gurgles, spinning her neck, and taking her mole with it.

Lorna scurries into her bedroom, to check on Darryl and squeal some more. The tears start again, on full-blast.

Perhaps this should've been mentioned earlier: they still live in the same house, Martin and Lorna. They've still got three months left on their contract, see, and at least a month's worth of electricity still left on the meter. While Lorna's desperate for Martin to move out (so she can have the house for herself), Martin's desperate to stay, in the hope that Lorna will be single again soon and he'll be perfectly poised (probably sat on the sofa downstairs) to snap her up again. As yet, things haven't gone to plan for either of them.

Martin's lungs play ping-pong with his heart, as he races down the rest of the corridor, to the landline. On the way past Lorna's bedroom, he can't resist sneaking a glance through the gap in her door. The wind-up merchant in his skull has already convinced him Lorna's new man must be at least 33% better looking than Martin, but he needs to know for sure. He cranes his neck, and squints.

As it turns out, Darryl's hardly a catch. He's got fresh third-degree burns covering his head and torso, a cricked neck, and no penis. Darryl lies sprawled, groaning, turning Lorna's white bed sheets red tie-dye. Lorna tries to dab his wounds with a fistful of Kleenex, but that just seems to hurt him more.

Martin smirks, inside himself. Walking onwards, he feels all-powerful again. He picks up the house-phone, and punches in 999. As he waits for the call to connect, he makes plans to get showered and change his socks, once Darryl's out of the building. And he makes plans to put the L doll in his bed tonight.

Later, as the ambulance carries Darryl away—with the sirens blaring, and Darryl's severed cock on ice—Martin gawps from the safety of his bedroom, crouching beneath his windowsill. He sees Lorna standing amongst the folk on the street corner, welling up again, with her dribbly left hand in her mouth. She watches the van leave through Vaseline lashes. She looks ever so heartbroken, herself.

This annoys Martin. He bites his lip anxiously. He hopes

he gets her back. He hopes to God she wasn't in it just for
Darryl's personality.

Dedicated to the lovelorn of Linthorpe, summer 2010.

Written by Toby Litt

THE FOOTNOTES

Illustrated by Rob Hunter

I keep, and have always kept, since age ten, a meticulous diary—and so I know the exact date and time that Guido and Paloma became footnotes.

We, the subject and I, were sitting on the verandah, looking out down across the familiar dried out fields and hills of our Tuscan view.

Oh dear, no—I should leave the description of landscape to others more qualified. Here is a sentence from a letter, unpublished: "The hill falls away from the house, gentle and stepped, in humping bumps, with the jerky rhythm of a child's toy falling downstairs."

The subject had just that morning had her first session with the official biographer. They had talked, in private, for just under three hours.

In order to be certain they wouldn't be interrupted, the biographer drove the subject across to a bar in a village two villages away.

Of a different generation entirely, how could this echo of the baby boom respond to the swing and syncopation of immediately post-war fiction?

Still, he came highly recommended—by his previous subject. "He's… keen to please," the elderly writer said, in a letter; a man who, to my certain knowledge, had enough skeletons in his literary closet to fill the Paris Catacombs.

They drove off, fast, in the baby blue Karmann Ghia, which wasn't the sort of car a real academic could afford.

While we were dressing for dinner that evening, the subject told me what they talked about.

"We established a structure," she said. "It will focus as much on the work as on the life, perhaps more." She smiled with grim delight. "I hope I'm dead before it comes out."

Of course I pooh-poohed this immediately, but the subject's wish was granted: she died a month to the day before the official publication date.

Some have said that she never recovered from reading the proof copy. That is nonsense: she read and corrected all the drafts, first to fifth. If anything killed her, it was that.

"It's going to be wildly academic," she continued, doing up her pearls—a gift from me. "There are going to be footnotes."

"Really?" I said. "I hope I'm going to merit more than that."

"Oh, darling Jean," said the subject. "You're going to be a whole chapter at least."

This pleased me. I wouldn't be a footnote, I would be a whole chapter at least.

The biographer, who reminded me of Larkin's Jake Balokowsky, would be returning the following morning.

Over dinner, it became clear that—following on from our conversation in the bedroom—the subject's mind had been playing with the notion.

"Guido," she said, "you'll be a footnote. And Paloma, too. Which is terrible to think of, really. Because there are so many people I'd prefer to forget who'll end up being chapters, or sections, even."

Sensitive as always, the subject noticed the delighted alarm on my face. "Not you, dear," she said, and patted my hand. Her liver spots were denser and darker than mine, a full ten years separating us. "Though your role mustn't be overstated."

And with that, the subject closed the subject and addressed herself to the gnocchi.

It was only with coffee—which I for once declined, in fear of sleeplessness—that the footnotes were mentioned again.

"Don't you think," said the subject, "that footnotes are really quite obvious. I mean, some young man—young writer—walks in here, and he just has footnote written all over him. It's as if he's got his dates printed across the front of his t-shirt. In fact, Peter is a bit like that, isn't he?" Peter, the biographer. "What do you think, Jean? Is he a line or a paragraph?"

"Well," I said, "he's very thin, isn't he?"

The subject laughed, and told me not to be so naughty.

She was radiant that evening, as she had been so often in the past, as she so seldom in the future would be.

"Call one of the footnotes to clear the table, and make sure they order eight bottles of wine for tomorrow. You know the sort I mean."

I did. I knew. I was a chapter.

The next morning Peter arrived for ten. This time, they decided to drive all the way to the city. I said that I would come, having some marketing to do. "But we'll go at the weekend," said the subject, "together. Today we're going to be hugger-mugger," she trilled, "and we can't be hugger-mugger if anyone else is there."

I saw Peter taking note of the Shakespearean allusion, before saying, "I think that's up to you." The sort of young man's sentence that means nothing at all.

Guido came out with the subject's sunglasses, which she'd left among the hats on the table in the entrance hall.

"Thank you, Guido," said the subject, then took hold of Guido's hand. "I insist that Guido be a footnote—a footnote at the very least. He's terribly important to me. I could hardly do without him."

Guido smiled in loyal pain.

"I'm sure Guido can be granted his full importance," said Peter, in Italian.

The subject kissed Guido's hand. "You see," she said. "I keep my promises."

So, in the end, did Peter.

"Guido Michelangelo," it read, "1915–2005. The loyal manservant of Mary's final, quiet years in Tuscany. Fought bravely for the allies in the Second World War, a period he was always reluctant to talk about. Grief-stricken at Mary's death, he retired from service to a life of contemplation."

Contemplating the bottom of a glass, or so I heard.

The official biographer's Karmann Ghia ripped off into the distance, leaving me behind with the footnotes.

The subject was not so chipper when she returned as when she departed.

She ran straight to her writing room, closed the door and was heard crying.

As I descended the stairs, a floorboard betrayed me.

"Please, whoever you are, go away."

She appeared in our bedroom, even redder-of-eye than myself, an hour before dinner.

"What is it?" I asked.

"We talked about my father," she said. "My lovely father."

She came over into my arms, and we dissolved into mutual consolation.

Dinner that evening was taken in our room. The subject said little and ate less.

"He was such a wonderful man," she remarked, just before we went to bed. "I was so scared of him, I hardly dared speak when he was in the room."

The next morning, the subject awoke dewy-eyed with

sleep's refreshment. "The worst is over," she said.

And in a way, it was. And in another way, it wasn't.

For the remainder of the month, days followed the routine that had already been established.

Sometimes the subject returned home giddy as a debutante, such as the afternoon they discussed publication of her first novel; sometimes it was tears, silence, the writing room and no dinner, as on as the evenings following husbands one and two.

"Oh dear," the subject confided to me, one night towards the end of the third week. "I had no idea I'd lived so long, or known so many unimportant people."

We laughed.

I was awaiting the day on which they would discuss me and my importance. I expected: the faithful and essential companion of Mary's silver and, so we hope, golden ages. At least.

The day did not come.

Peter arrived one morning (he was lodged in a nearby pensione) as teary-eyed as the subject had been the previous evening—the day's discussion having focussed on dear dead contemporaries. "I'm sorry. It's—" Peter said.

He didn't need to say any more.

The subject took him in her arms.

Acknowledgements: "Nor will I soon forget the compassion with which Mary treated my grief upon hearing of my mother's death."

I stepped aside—stepping, I think, at that moment, out of his text entirely.

Peter got into the Karmann Ghia, swore he was alright to drive and crashed into an olive tree before he'd reached the bottom of the hill.

We heard a bang, saw smoke rising, made Guido get the car out of the garage, drive us down.

The Karmann Ghia, beautiful car, was folded in two, like a baguette crammed into a too-small shopping bag.

Peter was trapped in there, somewhere.

We waited, smelling the petrol and thinking our lives were about to acquire a new worst.

Then it was over, and everything became again what it had been before.

With my assistance, Mary completed another novel, a late flowering, some say her best.

The only vestige of the official biographer's time were those we now habitually called footnotes, Guido and Paloma. Sometimes, too, when Mary kissed me, she called me Chapter Ninety-Nine.

When Peter returned, two years later, everything about him had changed.

He arrived in a local taxi, his crutches along with two suitcases on the roof rack. He brought a young woman with him, one with a bump under her frock.

We sat on the verandah, no hugger-mugger this time.

"I don't know if I can write it any more," said Peter. "Not as a straight biography."

His crutches were resting against the stucco wall, aluminium heating up in the summer sunlight.

"I hope you're not too disappointed," Peter said. "The publisher is quite happy. It's going to be more of a memoir-thing."

"An autobiography?" asked the subject with blithe curiosity.

"A study," said Peter.

He looked at me.

I've wondered ever since why, at this point, he chose to look at me.

"But will it have footnotes?" the subject asked.

"Oh, definitely," said the young woman with the bump —said the final short paragraph of the acknowledgements.

Contributors

Illustrators

Scott Campbell (Scott C)'s watercolor paintings can be found in magazines, comics, children's books, video games, and galleries around the world. Some of his most notable projects include the Great Showdowns series at greatshowdowns.com, Double Fine Action Comics at doublefine.com, the children's books *Zombie In Love* and *East Dragon, West Dragon* from Simon & Schuster, and the video games *Psychonauts* and *Brutal Legend* from Double Fine Productions.
PYRAMIDCAR.COM

Ian Dingman is an illustrator living in Oakland. His clients include The New York Times, Real Simple, Doubleday and The Boston Globe. He has exhibited work in Los Angeles, New York City, San Francisco and Washington D.C.
IANDINGMAN.COM

Carson Ellis was born in 1975 in Vancouver, Canada, raised in suburban New York and college-educated at the University of Montana in Missoula, where she recieved a BFA in Painting in 1998. She's the illustrator of many books, including *Wildwood* by Colin Meloy and *The Mysterious Benedict Society* by Trenton Lee Stewart as well as artist-in-residence for the band, The Decemberists. She lives in Portland, Oregon with Colin, her husband, Hank, her son, and Window, her weird cat.
CARSONELLIS.COM

William Exley was born in Sheffield, studied illustration in Brighton and has lived, worked and been a tourist in London since graduating. He uses a System 3 brush, spider black ink and a Wacom to draw, and finds distractions in comics, movies and podcasts about comics and movies.

WILLIAMEXLEY.CO.UK

Tom Gauld was born in 1976 and grew up in Aberdeenshire, Scotland. He works as a cartoonist and illustrator and is regularly published in the Guardian and The New York Times. His graphic novel *Goliath* is published by Drawn and Quarterly. He lives in London with his family.

TOMGAULD.COM

William Goldsmith is a UK-based illustrator. He is the author of the graphic novel *Vignettes of Ystov*, and is currently working on a follow-up book to be published by Jonathan Cape and Random House.

WILLIAMGOLDSMITH.CO.UK

Maxwell Holyoke-Hirsch is an illustrator based in New York.

HOLYOKEHIRSCH.COM

Robert Frank Hunter is a London based illustrator.

ROBERTFRANKHUNTER.COM

Oliver Jeffers makes pictures, paintings, drawings, and some other stuff. He tells stories, too, and has won a few awards. He is from Belfast in Northern Ireland, but now lives and works in Brooklyn, New York.

OLIVERJEFFERS.COM

Adrian Johnson is a Liverpool-born illustrator whose clients include Paul Smith, Adidas, Stüssy, Monocle, The New York Times and Unicef. He has exhibited work internationally and lectured at colleges and universities across the UK. He lives in Lewes, East Sussex with his wife and two children.
ADRIANJOHNSON.ORG.UK

Jim Tierney grew up in southeastern Pennsylvania, and studied illustration at The University of the Arts in Philadelphia. He worked as a cover designer at Penguin Books in New York for two and a half years. Now he lives and works in Brooklyn as a freelance designer, with his wife Sara Wood.
JIMTIERNEYART.COM

Hannah Waldron's work often explores the textures, patterns, forms and structures of her surroundings, and has an interest in the development of landscape over time.
HANNAHWALDRON.CO.UK

Writers

Joshua Allen is complex and exciting. He writes increasingly short stories on the internet.
FIRELAND.COM

Ned Beauman was born in London. He is the author of the novels *Boxer, Beetle* and *The Teleportation Accident*, and was named one of Granta's Best of Young British Novelists.
NEDBEAUMAN.CO.UK

Nicolas Burrows is an artist and musician from the British Isles, living and working in London. He is one-third of Nous Vous collective and makes music under the name Glaciers. So far he has published one small collection of writings and recorded two full-length albums, as well as various other odds and ends.
GLACIERS.BANDCAMP.COM / NOUSVOUS.EU

Michael Crowe is pretending someone else is writing this. In recent stories he noticed your bank statement slowly appearing as the sunrise, combined all Chinatowns to make a second China and suggested that Jupiter rotates in the opposite direction every time you say nah. He's 50% of Mysterious Letters.
MICHAELCROWE.ORG

Kevin Fanning is the author of *Jennifer Love Hewitt Times Infinity*. He lives in Cambridge, MA.
KEVINFANNING.COM / @KFAN

Toby Litt is best-known for writing his books—from *Adventures in Capitalism* to (so far) *Middle*—in alphabetical order; he is currently working on N. His headfuckfiction™ story "John & John" won the semi-widely-known Manchester Fiction Prize.
TOBYLITT.COM

Tess Lynch is a writer living in Los Angeles. Her work has appeared in Salon, The Morning News, Granta Online and GOOD magazine. She currently contributes to Grantland.
TESSLYNCH.TUMBLR.COM

Joe Meno is a fiction writer and playwright who lives in Chicago. A winner of the Nelson Algren Literary Award, a Pushcart Prize, and a finalist for the Story Prize, he is the bestselling author of six novels and two short story collections including *The Great Perhaps*, *The Boy Detective Fails*, and *Hairstyles of the Damned*. His latest is *Office Girl*, a novel.
JOEMENO.COM

Richard Milward was born in Middlesbrough in 1984. His novels *Apples* (2007) and *Ten Storey Love Song* (2009) were published to great critical acclaim by Faber, gaining accolades from Irvine Welsh ('a major talent') and Lauren Laverne ('astounding'). His latest novel, *Kimberly's Capital Punishment* (2012), is a sextuple-ended black comedy following a woman's disatrous foray into 'unadulterated altruism' in a nightmarish vision of Britain's capital.
RICHARDMILWARD.COM

Ronnie Scott is a contributor to The Believer and many Australian magazines, and the comics critic for ABC Radio National. In 2007, he founded The Lifted Brow, a freeform arts, culture, and fiction magazine.
RONALDDAVIDSCOTT.COM

Craig Taylor is the author of three books, including *Londoners: The Days and Nights of London Now—As Told By Those Who Love It, Hate It, Live It, Left It, and Long For It*. He is the editor of Five Dials magazine.
FIVEDIALS.COM/FIVEDIALS

Evie Wyld's first novel *After the Fire, a Still Small Voice* won the John Llewllyn Rhys prize and a Betty Trask award. Her second novel *All the Birds, Singing* was published by Jonathan Cape in 2013. Her short stories have been published in various magazines and journals including Granta and Vogue. She has also written various non-fiction pieces for The Observer, The Telegraph and the Guardian. She lives in London where she works in an independent bookshop called Review.

Staff

Jez Burrows is a designer, illustrator and woodland appreciator. He lives in San Francisco.
JEZBURROWS.COM

Ray Fenwick is an artist, illustrator and author living and working in Winnipeg, Manitoba, Canada.
RAYFENWICK.COM

Sean Michaels is the founder of the musicblog Said the Gramophone. His debut novel, *Us Conductors*, will be published in spring 2014; it is the story of Lev Termen, inventor of the theremin, and the search for his one true love. Sean lives in Montreal.
SAIDTHEGRAMOPHONE.COM

Lizzy Stewart is an illustrator who lives in South London where she draws stuff and teaches other people to draw stuff.
ABOUTTODAY.CO.UK

Acknowledgements

Scott Boms for typographic shepherding, Marteinn at Oddi for continued grace, Sam Winston for a long phone call, Bryony Quinn for notes and thoughts, and—above all—the writers and illustrators for their inexhaustible patience and generosity.

Colophon

You Are The Friction is set in Adobe Garamond Pro. It was designed in Edinburgh, London, Exeter, San Francisco, and the odd flight over the Atlantic Ocean.

Good guys win.